Three figures stepped from the building

The Executioner's face turned grim as he took in the gray body armor and helmets worn by the trio. Drawing his Beretta, he unleashed a three-round burst, hitting a Juggernaut in the helmet. The enemy staggered sideways, then tumbled out of view.

The remaining Juggernauts turned toward him, and Bolan fired again. The Parabellums slammed into the gray breastplate and the second man stumbled backward, but did not go down. The third gunner triggered his weapon as Bolan sprinted from the alley. He heard the projectiles buzzing around him, but he kept moving, seeking new cover. Diving behind a parked Escort, he crouched and fired another burst at the enemy, but failed to find the target.

A deafening silence followed, and Bolan raised his head, scoping the action before him. The Juggernaut had marched into the street, moving toward Bolan's position, determined to get a final telling shot at the warrior.

MACK BOLAN ®

The Executioner

DON PENDLETON'S
THE EXECUTIONER®
BODY ARMOR

A GOLD EAGLE BOOK FROM
W⊕RLDWIDE®

TORONTO • NEW YORK • LONDON
AMSTERDAM • PARIS • SYDNEY • HAMBURG
STOCKHOLM • ATHENS • TOKYO • MILAN
MADRID • WARSAW • BUDAPEST • AUCKLAND

First edition September 1997
ISBN 0-373-64225-3

Special thanks and acknowledgment to
William Fieldhouse for his contribution to this work.

BODY ARMOR

Printed in U.S.A.

Nought can deform the human race
Like to the armor's iron brace.

—William Blake, 1757-1827

Putting a man in armor does not make him a soldier.
War should not be about power, but rather the triumph
of good over evil. We cannot afford to forget that.

—Mack Bolan

THE

LEGEND

Nothing less than a war could have fashioned the destiny of the man called Mack Bolan. Bolan earned the Executioner title in the jungle hell of Vietnam.

But this soldier also wore another name—Sergeant Mercy. He was so tagged because of the compassion he showed to wounded comrades-in-arms and Vietnamese civilians.

Mack Bolan's second tour of duty ended prematurely when he was given emergency leave to return home and bury his family, victims of the Mob. Then he declared a one-man war against the Mafia.

He confronted the Families head-on from coast to coast, and soon a hope of victory began to appear. But Bolan had broken society's every rule. That same society started gunning for this elusive warrior—to no avail.

So Bolan was offered amnesty to work within the system against terrorism. This time, as an employee of Uncle Sam, Bolan became Colonel John Phoenix. With a command center at Stony Man Farm in Virginia, he and his new allies—Able Team and Phoenix Force—waged relentless war on a new adversary: the KGB.

But when his one true love, April Rose, died at the hands of the Soviet terror machine, Bolan severed all ties with Establishment authority.

Now, after a lengthy lone-wolf struggle and much soul-searching, the Executioner has agreed to enter an "arm's-length" alliance with his government once more, reserving the right to pursue personal missions in his Everlasting War.

1

Robbing banks just wasn't what it used to be, Mack Bolan thought as he listened to the criminals' conversation. He stood by the Pontiac Sunfire he'd parked in the dark alley, his laser microphone positioned on the metal lid of a trash container and aimed at a window of the Gossler Metal Products company.

The high-tech device cast a concentrated beam of laser light onto the glass pane, which was bounced off the surface to the receiver section of the unit. Sounds and voices were transmitted via vibrations, which Bolan caught by means of an earplug. A small recorder taped the conversation, as well.

Standing in a damp alley in a run-down section of Pittsburgh, Pennsylvania, to spy on a gang of bank robbers, wasn't the sort of mission the Executioner or those at Stony Man Farm usually handled. They specialized in taking on the most serious threats to the United States of America and the lives of the nation's citizens. Bank robbery didn't fit into that category. However, on the advice of some of his staff, the President had asked for Hal Brognola's help. The gang called themselves the Anarchists, and one of their leaders was a man named Joseph Hussein. There was the concern that the Anarchists might be a terrorist outfit, but that particular fear had been unfounded. It seemed that the gang had adopted their title more to frighten the public than with any genuine intention to overthrow the United States.

The Anarchists might not have been terrorists, but they had displayed considerable ruthlessness and brutality during the series of bank robberies that extended across four states. Half a dozen people had been killed by the hoodlums and twice that number injured. Bolan had been motivated by concern for future potential victims to take the mission: The Anarchists needed to be stopped, and so far local police and federal agencies had failed to do so.

Locating the gang's lair hadn't been difficult. Hussein had gotten a lot of attention due to his Arab background, but he appeared to be second-in-command to Red Stone, the outfit's actual leader. Born Rodney Stowallson, Stone had worked at the Gossler factory before the recession put the company out of business. He had turned to self-employment that landed him two years for armed robbery in Ohio.

The gang had already hit banks in Kentucky, Maryland, Ohio and West Virginia. Now Pennsylvania was their target, the abandoned metal products building their hideout.

Through the laser mike, Bolan caught the robbers arguing about money and where they should pull their next job. The Anarchists had already managed to collect an impressive total from the combined robberies—more than a million and a half dollars—but that was apparently not enough to satisfy their greed.

Different voices came over the mike, expressing concern about the risks they were running, wanting to leave the country before they were all killed or captured. Their fears were valid; there had been eleven original members of the gang, but two had been killed in shoot-outs with guards and the police. Bolan wasn't sure of the identities of all the surviving members, but two of them were young women, apparently thrill-junky friends of the hoods.

The Executioner was well prepared to teach them how high a price their actions carried. A Beretta 93-R pistol was holstered under his arm and an Uzi submachine gun waited on the front seat of the Pontiac. He also had a Ka-bar fighting knife attached to his belt, a wire garrote in a pocket of his black field jacket and plenty of extra magazines for his firearms. More weapons and supplies were stored in the trunk of the car.

Nine against one were serious odds, even for a combat veteran with Bolan's expertise and deadly hardware. The Anarchists had already shown that they were more than willing to use deadly force. The gang favored shotguns, as lethal as any automatic weapon at close range. The Executioner intended to do as much as possible to even the odds.

Detaching himself from the microphone, he moved to the trunk of the car and selected three grenades: two CS tear gas canisters and an M-26 fragmentation grenade. He also took a canvas case containing an M-17 mask to protect him from the effects of the tear gas. Finally he picked up the Uzi from the front seat, slinging it, the pistol grip readily available.

The Executioner emerged from the alley and headed for the factory, his blacksuit blending in with the shadows. There were no lights around the abandoned property, but his eyes had adjusted well to the darkness, and it provided plenty of concealment for his covert approach.

The factory gate was padlocked, but Bolan gained entry by simply slithering under a torn section of fence.

No sentry had been posted outside the building. The gang seemed extraordinarily careless to the soldier. Light flickered from a window on the second floor, and when he came upon two parked vehicles, he recognized the two-toned sedan that matched the description of the getaway car used in their last bank heist. They hadn't ditched the vehicle or even bothered to spray paint it.

He found a jimmied side door, its frame ravaged by a crowbar. With the Uzi leading, Bolan stepped over the threshold. He catfooted across the concrete floor toward a flight of metal stairs, his combat senses alert for any sign of the enemy, an alarm or trip wire.

Suddenly a voice bellowed from outside. "This is the police! We've got the place surrounded! Throw out your weapons and surrender!"

Bolan clenched his teeth and silently cursed. Stony Man had a link to the police computer mainframe, and there had been nothing to suggest that the Pittsburgh PD suspected the gang was using the factory for its hideout. They had to have been tipped off somehow, throwing together a strike unit on short notice.

Voices shouted and swore from the top of the stairs. Feet pounded the floor above Bolan's position, and he heard the metallic sound of pump-action shotguns being primed. The gang didn't sound as if it intended to surrender. Then two men appeared at the top of the stairs, shotguns in hand, flashlights bound to the barrels with duct tape. They snarled obscenities as they began to charge down the stairs.

The Executioner didn't wait for them to reach his position. Before their flashlight beams could detect him, he raised the Uzi and squeezed the trigger. The subgun's muzzle-flash filled the staircase with bright yellow light, and the leading Anarchist was hurled backward into his partner, his body slammed by 9 mm Parabellum rounds.

The second gunner pulled his shotgun's trigger, firing a burst of buckshot in Bolan's direction. The soldier hit the man with another salvo of rounds, splitting the guy's head. He tumbled down the stairs to form a graceless heap at the bottom.

Bolan removed a tear-gas canister from his belt, yanked the pin and hurled the explosive up the stairs at the remaining gang members. He then moved clear of the stairs, taking cover by a concrete pillar. He expected the enemy to respond to the Uzi fire, and they didn't disappoint him. Shotguns roared and buckshot rained down the stairwell, tearing into the corpses of their cohorts on the stairs.

The Executioner quickly donned his M-17 mask, as fumes of gas began to drift down the staircase. The furious gunfire ceased, replaced by coughing and wheezing from the enemy.

Before the Anarchists could recover, Bolan pulled the pin from the M-26 frag grenade, broke cover and hurled the bomb toward the enemy's nest. The M-26 exploded, and fragments of plaster and concrete showered down the stairs, along with the remains of another terminated member of the gang.

The Executioner charged up the steps. He had seized the advantage and intended to make the most of it. He reached the top of the stairs, triggering the Uzi even before he had a target. There were no innocent bystanders or hostages to worry about; anything that moved could be taken down.

Two figures moved. Both appeared to be seriously wounded by shrapnel, and Bolan took them both out with a 9 mm mercy round.

The soldier scanned the area. A number of sleeping bags lay scattered on the floor, and an overturned kerosene lamp leaked fuel.

Five members of the gang had been put down. The sound of gunshots alerted Bolan to the probability that the four survivors had found an escape route and were engaged in battle with the police outside.

The Executioner sprinted out of the building, gaining the alley. Movement by the garbage container drew his attention, and he swung his Uzi toward a dark figure. A heavily muscled man, his head dwarfed by a huge set of shoulders, shuffled forward. A shaggy mane of carrot-colored hair confirmed his identity. Red Stone had survived the grenade blast, but he hadn't escaped unscathed. Blood oozed down his bull neck, most likely from a ruptured eardrum. He gripped a Remington shotgun by the barrel, using the buttstock as a support. The two 12-gauge shells he held in his other hand suggested he'd been about to reload the weapon when the grenade had gone off.

Stone shook his head, still dazed, then his eyes

widened when he saw Bolan, clad in black, wearing a gas mask, a fearsome subgun in hand.

"You're finished," Bolan said. "Drop your weapon and face the wall."

Realizing Stone might have been deafened by the explosion, the Executioner shifted the Uzi to one hand, using his other to point to the ground. Stone glared at him, then cast down the shotgun shells. Suddenly he swung his other arm, hurling the Remington at Bolan. The weapon's heavy barrel crashed across the frame of the Uzi, striking the submachine gun from the soldier's grasp.

Stone's lips drew back in a snarl, and he charged before Bolan could reach for his other weapon. The Executioner had read the guy's file and knew Stone had held a championship title on a prison boxing team while an inmate at Ohio State Penitentiary. The burly ex-con obviously intended to beat Bolan to death.

The thug closed in fast, swinging a left hook at Bolan's head. The Executioner dodged his fist, slamming his right palm into Stone's forearm. Knocking his adversary off balance, Bolan hooked his left fist under Stone's extended arm, driving his knuckles into the man's solar plexus. Stone grunted with surprise and pain. Bolan quickly followed with a right elbow smash, landing a punishing blow to the side of his opponent's jaw. The big man staggered, and the Executioner drove his boot into Stone's knee.

Cartilage crunched in the joint, and the hardman stumbled. He steadied himself, his hand going to his belt. He whirled, lashing out with a large steel knife. The Executioner sprang back, just avoiding the vicious swipe of the blade.

"I'm gonna cut out your heart and spit on it!" Stone hissed through clenched teeth.

He tried to move in to accomplish his goal, but his dislocated kneecap hampered him, giving Bolan a split second to reach for the Beretta 93-R. But before he could unleather it, Stone swung his blade at the Executioner's arm. Bolan jerked his limb clear of the flashing steel, turning his body to the right. Stone's knife sliced air as the soldier managed to pull the Ka-bar from the belt sheath with his left hand. He thrust the knife in a jab-punch motion, striking the blade across Stone's forearm. The thug cried out as blood welled from the cut.

The Executioner's right hand quickly snared Stone's knife wrist, yanked him off balance and swung his left fist in a short, sideways stroke, driving the point of the Ka-bar under Stone's chin. The blade pierced the soft tissue at the hollow of the man's throat, then sank deep to puncture his windpipe.

Blood spurted, and Stone's eyes began to cloud over. Bolan released the man's wrist, and he crumpled to the ground.

The Executioner picked up his Uzi. "That leaves three," he said, moving on.

A TRIO OF POLICE CARS, their headlights blazing, formed a horseshoe pattern in front of the factory. Uniformed cops knelt by the vehicles, using them for cover as they exchanged gunfire with the remaining members of the Anarchists, who had taken shelter behind their own vehicles.

Mack Bolan emerged from the building to discover the battle in progress. The police clearly hadn't called for adequate backup, and they appeared to be armed with only handguns and shotguns. Since the gang members had the same type of weapons, neither side had the advantage of distance or accuracy.

The Executioner sized up the situation. He still had a canister of CS gas that he could lob at the enemy, then fire a few rounds at their position, letting the police know he was on their side. He would have to explain to them that he was working for the Justice Department, or some other federal outfit, get Stony Man Farm to back his story, then slip away before the lawmen could question him about using methods contrary to those generally employed by the Feds.

Suddenly, a vehicle charged onto the factory premises from the street. The bulky, box-shaped gray van hadn't slowed when it approached the perimeter fence, but had crashed into the metal barrier, bursting the hinges and hurling the gate aside.

Both the police and the Anarchists began to yell. Shotguns roared from the gang's position, buckshot ricocheting off the gray rig as it spun in a semicircle to come to a halt in front of them.

The van's rear door opened, and two figures stepped out.

The new arrivals moved away from the van, black helmets with dark-tinted visors concealing their faces. Their bodies were encased in dull gray suits of armor, with extra triangles of metal attached to the knee and elbow joints. Heavy black boots covered their feet, while their black gloves were studded with metal spikes on the knuckles and around the wrists. Side arms in flap holsters hung from their hips, and the belts held ammunition pouches. From their shoulder straps hung a weapon that resembled an old M-3 A-1 submachine gun, but the frame and barrel appeared thicker. An extra pistol grip had been mounted under the reinforced barrel.

Bolan flicked his gaze from the extraordinary pair to the police. They stood dumbfounded, as surprised as Bolan and the gang members. If the men from the van belonged to some sort of elite Pittsburgh SWAT force, the policemen didn't seem to know about it. The Executioner decided to stay behind cover, his Uzi held ready.

A female Anarchist braced her pump-action shotgun across the hood of the two-toned sedan and fired at the nearer armored figure. Her weapon roared, spitting fire. Pellets smashed into the center of the man's chest, yet he barely took a step back from the 12-gauge punch.

The startled gunner was working the action to her weapon when a short man appeared beside her. Bolan recognized Joseph Hussein. The Anarchist co-leader aimed a pistol at the armored pair. The .45-caliber Colt was a powerful, accurate weapon and a reliable man-stopper. Hussein triggered three rounds at the gray figures, hitting both of them, but the armored men barely reacted.

Bolan was surprised. He was familiar with Kevlar and other types of body armor, but he had never seen anything like this—armor that turned people into human tanks.

The woman shotgunner aimed her weapon and unleashed another burst of buckshot, with no more success than before.

The men in gray raised their weapons in unison.

Arms extended, fists clenched on the pistol grips by the trigger and barrel support, they opened fire, loosing a valley of shots. The woman was hurled backward, her long hair flying in all directions as her head was blown open.

The armored figures closed in on the Anarchists' vehicles in a determined, unhurried stride. Hussein desperately fired his .45 pistol. The pair responded with their subguns, and the robber dropped from view behind the sedan.

"Don't shoot!" a woman screamed.

The second female Anarchist, and the last member of the gang, stood slowly, her hands held above her head. She trembled, her face visibly pale in the available light as she stared at the armored gunmen.

"I give up."

One of the men in gray pointed his weapon at the woman, hitting her with a burst that almost decapitated her. The armored figures barely glanced at the corpses as they turned their attention to the sedan. One man opened the car's back door and climbed inside, while the other stood by, his weapon held ready.

"Jesus!" a police officer exclaimed as he advanced from his patrol car. "What the hell do you guys think you're—"

He stopped in midsentence as two more men clad in gray body armor and black helmets emerged from the back of the van, both pointing their subguns at him. His fellow officers thrust their riot guns and service revolvers over and around their vehicles, ready to back up their sergeant against the gunmen.

"Who are you?" the sergeant demanded. "Identify yourselves!"

The men in gray opened fire. A blast of bullets slammed into the sergeant, lifting him off his feet to land in a bloodied heap on the ground. The lawmen triggered their weapons in response. The rounds drilled into the armored shapes but didn't bring down either man. The helmeted foes sprayed the patrol cars with rounds, and Bolan saw a cop's head jerk violently before he fell.

The Executioner knew he couldn't stand by and watch the officers get slaughtered. Raising his Uzi, he took aim and scored a 3-round hit to the back of an opponent who was preoccupied with trying to kill more policemen. The guy lurched forward as if he'd been shoved, but he didn't go down. Bolan quickly switched targets, firing another burst at the second cop killer. He went for a head shot, slamming the enemy's helmet with a 9 mm Parabellum round. The man's head jerked to the side, and he spun from the impact, but it didn't take him down.

Movement by the sedan warned Bolan that the first two men were still in play. Both figures now stood by the vehicle, their visor-covered faces turned toward Bolan. Then one of them raised his subgun while the other attempted to get into the front seat of the car. The first gunman triggered a salvo of full-auto rounds at the Executioner, just as Bolan ducked, throwing himself behind the factory's stone doorframe. A bullet chipped stone from the corner of the frame, dislodging a chunk that hit the floor next to Bolan. He heard something punch through stone above his head and glanced up to see a dime-sized bullethole in the wall. The wall was at least eight inches thick, which should have been more than enough to stop bullets from penetrating.

The Executioner stayed low as he carefully peered around the corner. The armored gunman who had selected him for termination was marching forward, headed for the soldier's position.

Bolan knelt, and, using the doorframe for support, opened fire. He exhausted the last of the Uzi's magazine, nailing his adversary with at least five 9 mm rounds, from midtorso to the visor of his black helmet. The man jerked and staggered back a couple of steps, but then he came on, triggering a volley of autofire in response. Bullets hammered the doorframe around Bolan, while some rounds sizzled over his head.

Suddenly, the killer's subgun clicked on empty. He let it hang from the shoulder strap and clawed with his gloved hand at the holster on his hips.

Bolan also opted for his pistol rather than using valuable time to reload the Uzi. He drew the Beretta 93-R from shoulder leather with the speed and efficiency born of years of practice. The Beretta lacked the ammunition capacity of the Uzi, but Bolan knew he could fire the handgun with greater accuracy. That was of little comfort, since he hadn't been able to find an area of weakness in the enemy's suit of armor.

The gray assassin pulled a stainless-steel pistol from the hip holster. Bolan aimed the Beretta, trying to pick a target that would take out the enemy. He settled on his opponent's kneecap. The soldier had used that part of Red Stone's anatomy earlier, and it had helped him take out the burly Anarchist. Maybe a 9 mm stomp to the armored killer would do likewise.

Bolan targeted the sights on a triangle guard on his opponent's right knee, pushed the fire selector to 3-round-burst mode and squeezed the trigger. A trio of Parabellum bullets smashed into the target, sparking off the armor to confirm the hit. The hardman's leg swung out from under him, and he crashed to the ground. A sense of satisfaction rushed through the soldier when he saw his opponent finally go down, but that feeling was short-lived. Bolan realized that the killer had been hurt, not taken out of the game, as he fired his pistol from a prone position. Two bullets struck the wall by the doorframe, but neither round came close to the Executioner. The killer hauled himself to his feet, his free hand clutching his damaged knee as he fired the pistol again.

At that moment, the sedan tore over from the truck area, coming to a halt alongside the frustrated assassin. A helmeted figure sat behind the wheel. The gunman triggered another poorly aimed shot in Bolan's general direction before yanking open the vehicle's passenger-side door.

"You got lucky!" he bellowed, his voice distorted by the thick visor. "I'll get you next time!"

He climbed inside the car and it raced for the smashed front gate, followed by the gray van. As the rig approached the police vehicles, a grenade was hurled from its window. Policemen dashed from the projectile seconds before the bomb exploded. The blast tore apart one car, knocking another on its side. Gasoline ignited, sending flaming debris over the area. Both vehicles raced from the scene, leaving the police to fire a few useless rounds at the escaping rigs.

Bolan took advantage of the distraction to head for the gap in the fence. He would give chase in his own vehicle, try to catch up with the armored killers and try to figure out a way to take them out when he did.

2

Hal Brognola leaned back in his chair in Stony Man Farm's War Room. He chewed on his cigar as he listened to Bolan report on the incident in Pittsburgh. The big Fed's gaze narrowed more than once, and he nodded occasionally.

"I drove through the streets for a while," Bolan said, "but I didn't see either vehicle. There were a lot of police all over the place. I listened to the scanner and heard when they found the abandoned van and the sedan, but there was no sign of the armored men from the factory shoot-out."

"It sounds like a truck load of cyborgs arrived at the factory."

"They were human," Bolan assured him. "I was able to hurt one of them."

"You emptied an entire Uzi magazine into these guys, pulled the Beretta and fired more rounds, and all you managed to do was wound one of them?"

"Not exactly wound," Bolan replied. "The bullets didn't seem to pierce the metal knee guard. I might have broken his kneecap or maybe dislocated the joint."

"And they'd also been shot numerous times by both the police and the Anarchists?"

"Yeah. They nailed those guys with plenty of bullets and buckshot, but their body armor held up better than anything I've ever seen before. I've been shot when I was wearing a Kevlar vest. You get hit by a large-caliber slug or a shotgun blast, and the vest can save your life, but the impact will still knock you down. Those guys barely budged when they got hit. I even nailed two of them with head shots. The visor on the helmet seemed to be as sturdy as the armor."

Brognola leaned forward, punched a button on the console unit, then picked up a telephone handset and spoke into it.

"I'm glad you're still awake, Bear," he said. "It's about Striker's trip to Pittsburgh. We need you to tap into the police computers again. The district offices of the FBI and Justice as well, and maybe the Pennsylvania Highway Patrol while you're at it."

He listened for a moment as Aaron Kurtzman, Stony Man's chief of computer operations and high-tech Intelligence gathering, said something, then he went on.

"Yeah, I know the Anarchists were wiped out. The police say another gang took them out? That's sort of what happened. No, Striker's not who the police are looking for. Plug into those computer systems and you'll find out. I also want you to contact Kissinger. I want the Cowboy here, pronto. I'm not sure what's going on yet, Aaron, but we'll all find out together."

Brognola hung up. Bolan rose from his chair and walked to an office supply cabinet. He extracted a sketch pad and pencil, then returned to the table and began to draw the outline of a man.

"As our weapons' specialist, maybe Cowboy's

come across body armor similar to what you described, Mack,'' Brognola said.

Bolan continued to sketch, drawing the helmet, gloves and boots as precisely as he could.

''I doubt John's familiar with what I saw in Pittsburgh,'' he said. ''This is something new. The weapons they carried also packed some powerful ammunition. The bullets went through human flesh like an ice pick through tissue paper.''

''Okay,'' Brognola began, ''let's assume you're right and these guys wore superarmor with special hardware unlike anything to appear on the face of the earth before. So who are these guys? They weren't policemen and they weren't members of the Anarchist gang.''

Bolan glanced up at the Fed and shrugged as he spoke.

''When they shot down an unarmed woman who had clearly surrendered, I figured they weren't good guys. When they started to kill cops, I decided that officially made them bad guys.''

''But why were they there in the first place? I don't think they were just cruising the area and decided to join a shoot-out because they felt like killing some people for fun.''

''I wondered about that. They searched the sedan before they took the car. My guess is they found the million and a half dollars stolen by the Anarchists.''

''That's a nice bundle of cash,'' Brognola said, ''but they went to a lot of trouble and took on a mighty big risk to get that money.''

''Not as much risk as the bank robbers took to steal it initially. The men in the body armor seemed to have total confidence in their protective gear and weapons. They had good reason to feel confident, too.''

"Is there a reason why you didn't tell us about this through computer communications and waited to tell me face-to-face?"

"Yeah. I don't know who those guys are, what other sort of high-tech advantages they might have, or who they might be working for," the Executioner explained.

"Do you think they might have computer hacking ability and electronic devices advanced enough to listen to our satellite-secure transmissions?" Brognola asked with surprise. "You know we have state-of-the-art gear here at the farm. Even the CIA and the National Security Agency don't have anything more advanced. Are you suggesting that they're connected to a top-secret branch of the government, either an Intelligence agency or military?"

"They looked like they'd had military or paramilitary training," Bolan replied. "Learning to shoot a powerful automatic weapon takes time, and it's more difficult to handle a gun while wearing heavy gloves and a helmet with a visor. Ask any cop who's ever served on riot-control duty how that kind of gear reduces mobility and vision. These guys were familiar with their weapons and gear. Their tactics were simple, direct and violent. Go in, hit, grab what you want and get out. They could have done it faster and more efficiently, but they displayed a considerable arrogance about their invincible status. Unfortunately that proved to be justified.''

"If a branch of the government is involved, we'll find out," Brognola promised. "I'd also like to know how they knew the Anarchists were holed up in the factory. We had access to information about that location, and the police probably responded to a tip from somebody who saw the gang. The armor-plated hardmen were decked out for battle when they arrived, so they had to have been pretty sure they'd find the Anarchists.

"Anyway, before we jump through too many hoops, let's remember Stony Man is an organization that deals with extreme threats to the interests of the United States and the lives and safety of its citizens. Killing a bunch of bank robbers doesn't fit into that category. Gunning down those policemen is a serious crime, but it still isn't the sort of thing to constitute a genuine threat to the U.S."

"I realize this isn't a new mission and it might not be the sort of thing the Farm's been established to deal with, but I still think that what I saw could become a serious threat if it turns out to be more than an isolated incident."

Brognola nodded. "We'll look into this as a possible threat, but you know we can't put all our resources into a situation that doesn't fit our agenda. Stony Man isn't here to settle scores on an individual basis."

"I admit those body-armored troops shook me up a bit. Shooting guys who keep coming at you is pretty unnerving, Hal. But this isn't personal. These people are dangerous and ruthless, and I don't think this is the last we'll hear of them."

FIVE MINUTES LATER, Aaron Kurtzman rolled into the War Room, drew up to the conference table and handed Brognola a file. The big Fed glanced at the data and saw that it had been acquired from the computer center of the Pittsburgh PD and an FBI district office in Pennsylvania.

"It looks like they've got a three-state manhunt in progress to try to find the cop killers," he said.

"It may expand beyond that," Kurtzman replied. "You might want to check out a news story that will be on CNN in a few minutes. I came across it with a general Intelligence scan on the electronic information highway."

"How many police officers were killed or injured?" Bolan asked. "I saw two down with what looked like fatal wounds."

"Three are dead and one isn't expected to make it to dawn," Kurtzman answered. "Five others are hurt to various degrees. The police are baffled about how some of the Anarchists were killed inside the Gossler building when they didn't see any of the armored men enter the factory. Was that your handiwork, Striker?"

Bolan nodded. "Actually it happened before the armored assassins arrived."

"The cops are speculating that Joe Hussein might have been the one who took out Red Stone," Kurtzman said. "Everybody is sort of relieved the Anarchists are history, but they're pretty upset about those bulletproof guys. The FBI and some of the police brass suspect the story is an exaggeration. It's hard to believe that somebody gets hit by a shotgun blast at close range and still remains on his feet, regardless of what kind of body armor he's wearing."

"It's not hard for me to believe because I saw it," Bolan assured him. "Did they find the money?"

"Nope," Kurtzman answered. "A million and a half bucks still unaccounted for. The cops figure the armored guys got it. Of course, they don't know what happened to the group after they abandoned the Anarchists' sedan and the van they'd used for the hit. That vehicle turned out to be stolen from a newspaper distribution company less than eight hours prior to the incident. Steel plates, a battering ram pipe section under the fender and an engine shield had been welded onto the vehicle to reinforce the rig. They also slapped on a paint job and some Ohio license plates that are probably stolen. Whatever else can be said about these guys, they aren't lazy."

He turned his wheelchair slightly to aim the remote at a wall. He pressed a button on the unit, and a panel slid away to expose a wide-screen television set. He switched on the set and flicked the channels to CNN.

"Is the FBI sending a forensic team to investigate?" Brognola asked.

"I gave you the data sheets," Kurtzman complained. "Don't you guys ever read this stuff? Yeah, the Feds are sending a forensic unit. Ballistics, microfiber, blood and tissue, all sorts of fancy tests are supposed to be conducted. They also wanted to know if any of the police cars had video cameras installed. I suppose you want me to answer that question, too, instead of reading it for yourself?"

He went on without waiting for a response.

"One of the cop cars did have video. Guess which one."

"The car destroyed by the grenade?" Bolan said.

"That's right. It got blown to hell and the camera

with it." He turned to the television. "The top news stories are coming on, gents."

A pair of newscasters appeared. The middle-aged male, his silver hair carefully groomed, began to report the lead story.

"In Los Angeles, fourteen people are dead and twelve hospitalized after a violent incident at a location known to be a major crack house," he said. "Police suspect a rival drug gang is responsible for the carnage, but several eyewitnesses have expressed a different opinion. We go to Alan Chapman, reporting live from Los Angeles."

The scene changed to a man standing in front of a Los Angeles hospital emergency entrance. An ambulance stood by, and two orderlies hauled out a body on a stretcher.

"It's always busy here," Chapman began, "but tonight is more hectic than most. Victims of the violent gun battle at an alleged crack house are being treated here. There's no word yet on the condition of the survivors. Names of the dead and injured are being withheld until the next of kin have been notified, and all involved identified."

A run-down building of discolored brick appeared, yellow crime tape sealing off the area. Uniformed cops kept onlookers at bay, while body bags were carried from the building's entrance.

"This was the scene at the homicide site less than an hour ago," the reporter went on. "Apparently a group of heavily armed individuals, armor-clad and helmeted, appeared and conducted a bold raid. Authorities claim this site was well-known as a crack house, supplying crack cocaine to hundreds of customers every week. Some people in the neighborhood stated that the number of people going in and out of the building was higher than usual tonight. They also claim that a large group of men, described as criminal gang enforcers, were present. This didn't seem to deter the mysterious helmeted invaders. We go now to eyewitness reports.''

A middle-aged man appeared on the screen, and he spoke rapidly into a microphone.

"It sounded like there was a war in there, man. They were firing machine guns. I was in Nam, and I know what a machine gun sounds like. Bullets were shooting out windows, and people were screaming. I saw the flash of guns firing away inside. I expected grenades to go off or somebody to use a rocket launcher next. I've been in this neighborhood for years and I've seen a lot of this gang shoot-out stuff, but nothing like this. Nothing like this since Nam—"

He was cut off by a young woman. She pointed at the building with one hand as she spoke.

"They were cops, damn it! Cops dressed in riot helmets with some kind of bulletproof vests. They just marched in there and started shooting because they wanted to drive out the dealers and the junkies. Store owners probably called them in, merchants with friends in city hall wanting to push out the undesirable element. Who cares if they kill a bunch of drug addicts and dealers? That's what everybody thinks. So the cops come down here and make the local businesses happy by killing junkies instead of helping them get off crack."

She was replaced by a policeman.

"This was gang related," he declared. "I know

what some of these people are saying here, that cops did this. Maybe the gunmen did wear helmets and some kind of bulletproof vests, but that doesn't make them police officers. They were just a bunch of hoods killing each other over turf and drugs and money.''

"But isn't it true no drugs or money were found in the building?'' the reporter asked.

"That isn't exactly true. Some small containers of crack cocaine were found inside, but the large supply of drugs must have been taken by the rival gang, along with the cash that probably amounted to thousands of dollars. They ripped it off, and when we find them, we'll prove it.''

Once more, Alan Chapman appeared live by the hospital. His expression didn't reveal anything as he stared into the camera.

"Los Angeles has seen more than its share of gang violence associated with drug trafficking. Many people will try to convince themselves that this sort of deadly invasion can only occur in a crack house or a high-crime neighborhood. Yet, the citizens of Los Angeles have seen how violence can spread, and no one can really feel safe when bands of killers with military assault weapons roam the streets of this city. This is Alan Chapman reporting from Los Angeles.''

Aaron Kurtzman turned to the Executioner and asked, "Does this sound like the guys you encountered in Pittsburgh?''

Bolan nodded. "They must have hit that crack house in L.A. about the same time as the strike on the Gossler factory,'' he said.

As if to confirm his statement, the CNN broadcast went on to discuss the incident in Pennsylvania. Although the news report declared that the Anarchists had apparently been destroyed and both ringleaders killed, no mention was made of the helmeted attackers. An unspecified number of police officers had been killed and others injured. There was also an unconfirmed story that some of the gang members, or perhaps a rival gang, had escaped a police barricade. Details hadn't been released to the press.

"They won't be able to sit on this for long," Brognola said. "News about identical gunmen in helmets and body armor in both Pittsburgh and Los Angeles is going to stir up a real hornet's nest. What the hell is this, Mack? Some sort of nationwide vigilante outfit with advanced protective gear and some kick-ass weapons?"

"I'm not sure what's going on, Hal," Bolan answered, "but I think we'd better look into it. Figure you can spare some Stony Man personnel for a couple of days?"

"We've already called in Kissinger. We'll see about getting him on the FBI forensics unit as a weapons and ballistic expert. Leo Turrin can use his status with the Justice Department to check out L.A. Maybe you'd like to go along with him. We'll have a Justice ID and pistol permit ready for you tomorrow."

"Okay," Bolan agreed. "I'll stay here tonight. I'll just wait for the Cowboy to get here. I want to make sure he has something ready for me before I head for California. Some special ammunition with armor-piercing bullets."

3

The dog twisted and convulsed beneath the net of metal mesh. Andrew Gallow watched emotionlessly as the stench of burned fur and the crackle of electricity accompanied the frantic movement of the animal. He frowned as the dog gave a final twitch, then lay still. Sighing, he glanced at the remote-control unit in his hand and limped across the tiled floor to a work bench in the research section. Childhood polio had left his right leg partially paralyzed. He had been unable to participate in sports as a boy, and his desire to serve in the military or in law enforcement had also been denied him. He had tried to compensate for his physical limitation by using his mind and mechanical talents to pursue his goals.

Extremely near-sighted as well, Gallow wore glasses with thick lenses that contributed to the "nerd" image he had resented his entire life. Adjusting his glasses on the bridge of his nose, he used a narrow screwdriver to remove the back plate from the remote unit.

"Jesus," a voice remarked, "what's that smell?"

Gallow glanced up at Raymond Stylles. Tall, athletic and blessed with superb health and 20/20 vision, Stylles was the sort of man Gallow had always longed to be. A former soldier, police officer and special agent with the FBI, Stylles had led an active and exciting life. Gallow could never suppress a feeling of envy whenever the man was around him.

Stylles wrinkled his nose at the offensive odor as he glanced about the room, his eyes falling on the charred corpse of the dog under the net.

"I was testing a new stun net," Gallow explained. "The electrical charge seems to be too high."

"No kidding," Stylles said. "It looks like you barbecued that animal, Andrew."

"It's a tricky business, electricity. If it isn't strong enough, it won't disable your opponent, and if it's too strong, it'll fry him."

"Still, better too much than too little," Stylles declared. "The safety of the law-enforcement officer should always be considered over the well-being of a low-life criminal who has to be restrained."

"You know I feel the same way," Gallow said. "This net is designed to help handle suspects who are unarmed and who present a lesser threat to law-enforcement personnel. Like a violent drunk, for example. It's still in the experimental stage, though."

"If you keep experimenting like that, you'll run out of dogs pretty soon," Stylles said.

Gallow sighed. "That was my last one," he said. "The stun net can wait, anyway. It's just a side project I've been working on. Any word on the rest of the L.A. team?"

"Yeah. They left California and they're making their way across country. We don't want them breaking any speed limits. The last thing we need is to have some cop decide to search one of those vehicles. No way they can explain why they're carrying your miracle body armor, let alone the stacks of money, bundles of drugs and those fancy firearms.''

Gallow smiled with satisfaction. ''Everything worked well in the field,'' he said, ''didn't it?''

''I took a plane back here so I could tell you in person, as soon as possible,'' Stylles replied. ''Your inventions worked even better in the field than we expected. Those crack-dealing scum never had a chance when we hit their place. You should have seen their faces. When they first saw us they just stood there with their mouths hanging open.''

''They must have been even more surprised when they fired their weapons at you,'' Gallow said. ''What was it like, Ray? How did it feel to be indestructible?''

Stylles smiled as he spoke. ''I felt like a god, Andy. One of them fired an Ingram MAC-10 point-blank at my chest. The bullets hit the breastplate, and all it felt like was getting poked by someone's fingers. I enjoyed that sense of power so much that I didn't even shoot back. The dumb bastard ran out of ammo for his weapon and he just stood there, frozen with fear. I didn't want to waste a bullet on him, so I hit him with a left hook instead.''

''With the cestus glove,'' Gallow said.

''Exactly. I caught him on the side of his face with those steel spikes. The punk's teeth came out like a mouthful of bone chips and his jaw dangled, broken and useless. When he fell to his knees, I hit him again, nailing him at the base of his skull. Snapped his spinal cord right by the brain stem. Two punches, wham-bam, and he was dead.''

"But they couldn't touch you."

"They tried. They fired handguns, shotguns and a number of automatic weapons at us. I have to admit I was sort of scared when one of them pointed a gun right at my face and opened fire. The visor held up beautifully, though. The bullet didn't even scratch it."

"And the guns?" Gallow asked, like a child urging a parent to continue with a favorite story. "They worked well, too, didn't they?"

"They were great," Stylles confirmed. "The bullets punched through them like they were made of cream cheese. I brought down three punks in a narrow corridor by shooting into the first guy. The bullets went right through him and the two guys behind him. It was the most thrilling experience I've ever had, Andy. One of these times you'll have to come along with us on a raid."

"I'd sure like to," Gallow said with a sigh, "but with my leg and my poor eyesight—"

"You can still join us. You don't have to be able to run or even walk fast. They can't hurt you even if you just stand there and let them try."

"Not quite," Gallow corrected him. "Jurgens suffered a broken knee in Pittsburgh. One of those Anarchists managed to shoot him directly in the joint guard with at least two high-velocity rounds."

"Pretty impressive marksmanship," Stylles said. "I didn't think any of those bank-robbing morons were capable of that sort of shooting."

"Whoever the shooter was, he was the only one to get away. St. John had to pull out before they could hunt him down."

Stylles frowned. "But all the Anarchists have been

accounted for," he said. "The FBI knew the names of all its members. They had been identified from photos taken by bank security cameras. Every member is dead."

"Well, they weren't all killed by our people," Gallow stated. "They only took out three. The others must have been killed by the police. It's ironic that our people wound up having to kill more cops than robbers during that raid. How could we have guessed a bunch of idiot cops would try a cowboy hit on the Anarchists at the Gossler factory?"

"They obviously wanted to show the Feds how good they were at their job," Stylles remarked. "I've seen that plenty of times in the past. There's not much you can do when people allow their stupidity to get them into a situation that results in their death."

"St. John took it pretty hard. He didn't like the fact that cops were killed. He considers them fellow soldiers, on the same side of a war against crime and the destruction of our nation."

"I'm sorry it happened too, but he should realize good men get cut down by friendly fire in almost every major conflict."

"You can tell him that yourself," Gallow suggested. "He and the others from the Pittsburgh assignment arrived while you were taking your shower. They got the money, nearly one and a half million dollars. A nice addition to our war chest."

"We'll have more coming in, Andy. There's a lot of dirty money out there, waiting for us to confiscate for a worthy cause. Stupid legislation has kept law enforcement from doing this to finance operations against organized crime. Damn big-shot hoodlums make a fortune selling drugs and with other crooked deals while law enforcement is saddled with restricted budgets and pathetic regulations.''

"And those rich crime lords have been able to count on high-priced lawyers and a convoluted legal system to avoid punishment," Gallow added. "But they won't be able to protect them from the justice of the Juggernauts."

"Juggernauts?" Stylles asked with raised eyebrows.

"Yes. As it means an indestructible force that crushes everything in its path, I thought that it would be a good name for our troops."

"I like it," Stylles said. "You feel like a juggernaut in that body armor, armed with a gun that can blast through a brick wall. Nobody can stop you and you can kill anything that gets in your way. If that doesn't make us Juggernauts, I don't know what will."

ZACHARY ST. JOHN DROVE his fist into the makawara board. He struck repeatedly, using the knuckles on his fore and middle fingers in a classic karate punch, setting the rope-bound pad rocking.

Gallow and Stylles watched him go through his routine, alternating his punches with a series of kicks.

"You didn't see enough action last night?" Stylles inquired as he approached the man.

St. John turned to face the pair. Lean, strong and fast, he was a veteran fighting man. A former captain with the Airborne Rangers, he was a natural leader, and his military expertise made him a valuable addition to their organization.

"Maybe I just need to burn off some nervous energy," he replied, "or some anger."

He padded barefoot across the lawn to join Stylles and Gallow. The trio strolled across the patio, entered the building and made their way to Gallow's office. The inventor limped to his desk and perched on the corner to face St. John.

"So tell us what you're angry about, Captain," he suggested.

"I find killing police officers distasteful to say the least," St. John said, "but I'm not going to dwell on that too much. I've gone over that scene at Pittsburgh in my mind and I don't see any other way we could have handled it. I do have another problem, though. I really don't like the idea of us getting into the drug business."

"Who said we were getting into drug trafficking?" Stylles inquired.

"News reports stated that large amounts of the drug supply had apparently been stolen during the raid at the crack house in Los Angeles. You telling me this isn't true, Ray?"

Stylles sighed. "We need to raise more money to fund our Juggernaut Brigade. Leaving that coke behind would be like turning our backs on a million dollars."

"By selling that poison on the streets?" St. John demanded. "I thought our goal was to crush these filthy drug dealers. Now, you say we're going to join them."

"Our goals are considerably higher than simply putting some cocaine dealers out of business," Gallow said. "We might have to bend our principles a bit to accomplish those goals, but the results will compensate for whatever extremes are necessary.''

"Selling drugs is a bit more than bending principles in my opinion,'' the former Airborne Ranger said.

"We don't have to get involved,'' Stylles told him. "I know some people who will take care of this, a small but ambitious group of lawbreakers who will jump at a score like this. They won't be able to pay us what it's worth, but we can sell them part of the score now and the rest later after they've earned more cash.''

"By selling more damn drugs to children in school yards,'' St. John said.

"We're not responsible for who they sell the drugs to,'' Gallow stated. "Somebody will sell the stuff anyway. At least we'll make a profit from it.''

"And that makes it acceptable?'' the captain asked. "Then how are we any different from the people we're opposed to?''

"The difference is the reason we're doing it and what we'll do with the money,'' Stylles insisted. "What do you think would have happened to that cocaine if we'd left it? Someone would have gathered it up and tried to sell it, unless a bunch of junkies found it and decided to take the stuff for their own personal consumption.''

"The police arrived shortly after you left the area. They would have confiscated the drugs.''

"And there would have been a fifty-fifty chance it would have been surreptitiously removed from the evidence room by cops willing to increase their income by pushing some dope on the side. You'd be surprised how many of those narcotic plastic bags in the evidence rooms of police departments across the country are fakes. Somebody takes the drugs and replaces part or all of it with sugar, baking powder, or whatever looks the same," Stylles said.

"Then of course cops use informers," he went on. "Prostitutes, drug addicts, or a combination of the two. These low-level criminals give information for pay or for some sort of favor. The cops know these junkies use the payoffs to buy drugs. Frequently they look the other way when they catch these informers with narcotics, or blackmail them with the threat of arrest if they don't agree to help them. Some even directly supply the addicts with drugs."

"I'm afraid this is one old country boy who finds that practice to be unsavory. I know that the police use these informers to go after higher-ranking bad guys, but do you really think that's the same as us dealing with crack pushers to make money?"

"To finance our operation," Gallow corrected him. "Look, Captain. You're an honorable man and I appreciate that, but you must realize we don't live in an honorable world. If we did, none of us would be here and there'd be no need for the Juggernaut Brigade. The governments of several countries have been directly involved in drug trafficking, from the British who launched the Opium Wars against the Chinese emperor when he tried to stop production of the drug, to the KGB who smuggled heroin into the West to try to further corrupt Western culture, like we needed help to do that."

"I'm aware of all that," St. John stated, "but we're not British monarchs or damn Communists."

"The U.S. government has been involved in this too," Stylles picked up. "The CIA and NSA have participated in the trafficking of heroin and cocaine from Southeast Asia, Central America and Afghanistan. It was usually done in the name of supporting some anti-Communist movement, or a so-called noble cause like raising funds for the Contras in Nicaragua. It's all part of the politics of narcotics. It's a dirty game, but right now we have to play it, Zach."

"I still don't like it," St. John said, shaking his head. "When we establish our army as a national organization there won't be any more of this business with drug dealers. That's got to come to an end. We've got to concentrate on purifying this country, and we can't do that if we remain impure ourselves."

Gallow nearly laughed in the captain's face. Did he really believe power had anything to do with purity? One took control any way possible and stayed in control by doing whatever was necessary.

Stylles's expression was serious as he nodded and addressed St. John. "When we reach our goal, we'll crush every damn dope dealer and user in the United States," he assured the man. "Hell, the group I'm using as our go-between will be the first to get the ax. They could prove to be an embarrassment if news of us having used them ever became public knowledge. We use them now, then get rid of them when we don't need them anymore."

"Well, I'm going to try to not even think about them for now," St. John said. "What's our next move, gentlemen?"

"What else do you do with a juggernaut force that can't be stopped?" Gallow asked with a grin. "We go for another target. We have a couple of possible sites. We can go for two at the same time, or just hit one."

"Let's check them out first, then we can figure out what to do," Stylles suggested.

"All right," Gallow replied. "By the way, if any of our men make a trip to get supplies, let me know if they'll be passing a dog pound."

4

"Oh, great, two agents from the Department of Justice," Captain Ryder said. "I can't tell you how thrilled we are to have more Feds help us with our investigation."

Mack Bolan closed the ID folder that claimed he was Special Agent Michael Belasko. He hadn't expected a warm welcome from the Los Angeles police. He glanced at Leo Turrin. The little Fed's expression displayed no surprise that the police were annoyed with outsiders poking around their turf. He knew how territorial cops were, and Ryder seemed to be more so than most.

"So far we've got the DEA, the BATF and the FBI trying to tell us how to do our job," Ryder complained. "All of you throwing your weight around with that high and mighty federal government attitude. It's bad enough we've got the media on our backs asking what we know about that crack house slaughter. Most of them want to know if any of our people have helmets and protective suits that might fit what the eyewitnesses claim they saw last night."

Turrin sank into a chair by the desk and looked at Ryder with genuine sympathy. The Fed had formerly been undercover with the Mob and he'd found federal outfits a real pain at the time. Of course, he hadn't been terribly fond of local cops back when he was on the opposite side of the law, either.

"You know, Captain," Turrin began, "we didn't come here to ruin your day. We don't think the LAPD has some sort of death squad carrying out raids on crack houses, or that you guys are lying down on the job."

"That's mighty big of you," Ryder retorted. "What did you say your name was again? Was that a misprint on your ID or is that really your name?"

"Yeah. Leonard Justice. Justice with Justice," Turrin replied. "It's easy to remember that way."

"I'm not sure I should be talking to you guys until I get some confirmation from your superiors at Justice, back in Washington," Ryder said.

"I don't think we have time to waste," Bolan said, reaching inside his jacket pocket and drawing out a sheet of paper. He unfolded it to show Ryder his sketch of a gunman clad in body armor, head encased in a visored helmet, and holding a strange weapon. Ryder stared at the drawing, his eyes wide.

"Is this similar to what witnesses claim they saw at the crack house?" the Executioner asked.

Ryder nodded and turned his gaze to Bolan. "Where did you get that sketch?"

"It's based on the description from an eyewitness of another incident," Bolan answered. "We think there may be a connection."

"None of the other Feds said anything about this."

"That's because they don't know about this possible connection," Turrin explained. "And we'd like to keep it that way for now, Captain. Right now, we don't even know if we trust our fellow Feds. Isn't that ironic?''

"So why would you trust me?" Ryder asked.

"We'll just have to take a chance," Turrin answered. "We're still gathering facts about what's going on. We sure could use your help, Captain.''

"Well, I can tell you that a number of witnesses claimed the men who attacked that crack house were dressed like this figure in the sketch,'' the captain said. "You think some branch of the federal government might have gone into the vigilante death squad business? Just like those *federale* assassination groups down in Central America?''

"We can't say that," Bolan replied. "We know the FBI is assisting with ballistics, but your forensics people were at the scene first. We'd like to see what they've got so far concerning the bullets found at the crack house. Other lab results from prints, tire tracks, clothing fibers and so on would also be appreciated, Captain. You may also have reports of suspicious persons or vehicles in the area around the time of the raid that may be worth looking into, although your people are probably the best to evaluate that sort of data because they know the city and have a feel for what goes on in the streets.''

"I can have most of that information for you in about an hour," Ryder assured him. "Right around lunchtime. You guys got an expense account for this trip?''

"Lunch is on us," Turrin replied. "Actually on the taxpayers, but they won't notice. I know you're going to call D.C. to check on us between now and then. Just keep those details confidential. They'll fax you data and photos to verify who we are, so don't burn our security. See, we're not even sure if we can trust everybody in Justice at this point.''

"Jesus,'' Ryder said, "how big is this, Justice?''

"Call me Leo,'' Turrin said. "It doesn't sound so dumb. We don't know how big it is, but it has some people worried who don't usually scare so easy, people who are used to taking on some major threats to our national security.''

"Then this isn't just a gang war?''

"That depends on what you call a gang,'' Bolan replied. "This may be the first skirmish of a war. We're just trying to keep this thing from blowing into a conflict that won't benefit anybody except the manufacturers of body bags.''

RYDER PICKED the restaurant for lunch, an expensive seafood place called Neptune's Feast. Fishing nets dangled from the ceiling and draped the walls, which were adorned with seashells, dried starfish and driftwood. A huge marlin was mounted above the mirror behind the bar. The tables resembled giant clams with carved seahorses for legs, while a revolving blue light tried to create the impression of being underwater.

A waiter dressed in a sailor suit took their order and headed for the kitchen. Ryder seemed in better spirits, more relaxed.

"You like this place, huh?'' Turrin inquired as he glanced uncomfortably about the restaurant.

"Do you have some information for us?'' Bolan asked the captain, getting down to business.

Ryder opened a briefcase and removed a folder that

contained several reports. He donned a pair of wire-rimmed glasses and scanned the first sheet.

"Okay," he began, "early ballistics report. They found bullets all over the crack house. They fished slugs out of the walls, ceiling, furniture, floorboards and the bodies of the dead and wounded. A lot of different calibers were used in the gun battle. Many appear to have belonged to the drug dealers. They pack some pretty heavy hardware these days in L.A. You can buy anything short of a tank on the black market. The pushers had Ingram MAC-10 machine pistols, a couple of M-16 assault rifles, some shotguns and a variety of handguns."

"Sounds like they turned the place into an armed fortress," Turrin remarked.

"They did," Ryder confirmed. "Off the record, the narcotics division knew about the place, but they hadn't tried to bust the house because the bad guys had such a big arsenal. They planned to launch a raid when they could get together enough firepower, but your friends in the funny suits and helmets beat us to it."

"Anything unusual about any of the slugs they studied?" Bolan asked.

"Dozens of misshapen bullets were found. Forensics says these appeared to have struck some sort of solid object. Real solid. It looked like the slugs had slammed into a sheet of steel at least three inches thick."

"Body armor that thick?" Turrin asked, looking at Bolan. "Is that possible?"

"Maybe," Bolan replied, "but that would be a lot

of weight to haul around. Any information on the killers' weapons?''

''I have a special note on that,'' Ryder said. ''It says here that all the victims were apparently killed by weapons of a high-velocity caliber. Rounds were specially designed, unlike anything our forensics people have seen before. Most of these slugs were distorted, although they seemed to have punched through walls, furniture and human flesh with ease. When they finally hit their mark, they were pretty mangled. Forensics thinks they might be 10 mm or maybe .41 Magnum rounds, but these are hot loads, superhot. They've never come across anything like this before and, believe me, they've seen a hell of a lot, working crime scenes in this city.''

''No idea about the weapons' make or model?''

''Not really. The number of rounds suggests the weapons must be full-auto or maybe semiauto. Velocity of the bullets and groove marks suggest a barrel length of a foot or more. By the way, two of the victims were actually beaten to death—faces, heads and rib cages smashed in as if by a sledgehammer. A hammer with big steel studs, from the description of the wounds.''

''The gloves,'' Bolan stated. ''Metal gauntlets with spikes. A fist with a cestus like that would be a war hammer at close range.''

''A cestus? What's that?'' Ryder asked.

''Boxers in ancient Rome used to wear leather straps around their fists, often weighted with lead or studded with iron spikes.''

''They used to box with brass knuckles?'' Ryder

said. "They must have had some bloody messes in the ring back then."

"I think that was the idea," Turrin commented. "They liked some blood and gore with their entertainment in Rome. So what else did forensics come up with?"

"Footprints on the stairs they think were those of the killers. Seems they all wore the same type of heavy boot with a thick rubber sole that had a wafflelike pattern. None of these guys were little. The smallest boot was a size ten-and-a-half, the biggest a size fourteen."

"Big Foot in body armor," Turrin mused. "What about tire tracks?"

"I got them, too. They found some tracks to a large automobile, probably a four door, and a van-style truck. I think we found them abandoned outside town. Turns out the vehicles were stolen in San Diego and supplied with Arizona plates. They were also customized."

"Reinforced metal in the body, battering ram welded under the front fender and a shell over the engine?" Bolan asked.

Ryder nodded. "That's right. You want to tell me how you knew that?"

"It fits the previous MO of another hit," the Executioner said. "These guys are resourceful as well as dangerous. So far we haven't been able to catch them making too many mistakes."

"I don't know that they made a mistake hitting that crack house," Ryder said with a shrug. "You know, the people killed at that place were the scum of the earth. You guys ever see what crack does to people?

The addiction burns them out and fries their brains. The bastards sell it to school kids. Those drug gangs are armed to the teeth with better weapons than we cops have. They're crazy animals who don't give a damn about human life, not even their own. They'll kill an innocent bystander or a cop without hesitation. Sorry if I can't get too choked up about slime like that getting taken down.''

Bolan turned to face the captain. He understood Ryder's anger and frustration, knowing better than many men the desire to hunt down evil and blast the life from it.

''Before you start to think the men in the body armor are some sort of noble vigilantes,'' he said, ''you should know they've already killed at least three police officers. They may not be on the same side as the dealers they killed and stole from, but they're not on our side, either.''

''So who the hell are they and what do they want?'' Ryder asked.

''That's what we're trying to find out,'' the Executioner assured him.

5

Mack Bolan placed the laptop computer on the desk of the hotel room. He opened the lid and punched in the access code to a special security line with a communications satellite used exclusively by Stony Man personnel. Leo Turrin unpacked his garment bag, concerned that the "Fed suits" for the trip might be wrinkled. Aside from color, the single-breasted, off-the-rack outfits were identical in style and design. Turrin believed they added an official quality to his appearance, yet his taste for wide, flashy neckties often undermined the serious image he tried to present.

"Can you believe that restaurant Ryder picked?" he asked. "They ought to change the name of the place to Sissy Seafood. You'd never see cops in New York hanging out in a place like that. Not in Chicago, either."

Bolan had heard similar complaints from Turrin. California had become one of his favorite targets. The Executioner didn't answer, concentrating on establishing the communications link with Stony Man Farm, aware Turrin was just voicing his annoyance because he didn't have enough to do at the moment.

"You know, every time they send me to this state," the little Fed continued, "it's more crazy than the last. Psycho street gangs, wimpy cops and trials that unfold like soap opera plots. It's all too much.

"You notice all the disasters that have been happening here in the past couple of years?" Turrin went on. "The earthquakes, mud slides, riots, and either a drought one year or a flood the next. You know what I think, Mack?"

"You figure it's some kind of message," Bolan replied without bothering to look up from the screen. "A warning to California to change its ways."

"Yeah. How'd you guess?"

"Spooky, isn't it?" Bolan replied.

The Farm came on-line. Colors swirled on the screen and materialized into real-time broadcast from Stony Man HQ. Hal Brognola appeared, seated at the conference table in the War Room, John "Cowboy" Kissinger standing behind him.

"Hello, Striker," Brognola said. "How are things in California?"

"I'll let you talk to Leo about that later," Bolan replied. "I didn't expect to see the Cowboy back from Pittsburgh this soon."

"The FBI sent evidence to Quantico," Kissinger explained. "I headed there to examine it and the lab reports. I just got back a few minutes ago. You were right, Mack. There's something very different about these people running around in body armor."

"I appreciated that when I saw them in action," Bolan said. "The LAPD seems baffled by the case. They say the bullets used are unique armor-piercing projectiles, but they're not quite sure what caliber."

"Ten millimeter," Kissinger declared. "That much has been confirmed at Quantico. The make and manufacture are unfamiliar and the FBI hasn't been able to determine where these bullets are made. The metals used are also very unusual. Tungsten and rhodium are among the chief alloys used, and the tips are coated with a hard plastic similar to something developed by NASA for the space shuttle.''

"NASA?" Turrin asked with surprise as he leaned over Bolan's shoulder.

"It's similar to a spacecraft plastic," Kissinger explained, "but that doesn't mean we have a real lead there. Anyway, these are some kick-ass 10 mm rounds. Those Pittsburgh cops wore bulletproof vests, but the bullets punched right through them. Obviously these are superhot loads. You say the guns they used resembled M-3 grease guns, Striker?"

"That's what came to mind when I saw the weapons," Bolan answered. "The barrel and frame were thicker, though, and the cyclic rate seemed slower."

"Well, the old M-3 never was much for high cyclic rate," Kissinger said. "The maximum was maybe 450 rounds per minute, and even then it suffered from serious control problems that reduced accuracy."

"Yeah," Bolan agreed, "but the weapons these guys used seemed to be even slower than 450 rpm. That might be to help control the weapon when it fired such powerful ammunition."

"The blowback action might be modified."

"I'm sure it is. Everything on the gun appeared to have been reinforced and altered. The heavy ribbed barrel would cut down on muzzle-climb. That was always a major problem with the M-3."

"True," Kissinger agreed. "The best thing to be said about the M-3 is that it had a simple design. Not too many parts, easy to break down and reassemble. Maybe somebody took the old design, looked at what was wrong and decided to make improvements.''

"I'm sure you two are having fun discussing firearms,'' Brognola broke in, ''but it all comes down to the fact that these guys are using some new kind of gun. Right?''

"Pretty much so,'' Kissinger replied. ''The weapons and special ammunition would be impressive enough, but the body armor they have is even more amazing.''

"Has the FBI been able to come up with anything on it?'' Bolan asked. ''All the L.A. forensics people have are some mangled bullets that seemed as if they'd slammed into a thick steel wall.''

"Yeah,'' Kissinger said with a nod. ''A lot of the slugs recovered at the Pittsburgh site sort of looked like that, too. They hit something damn hard, but it wasn't a wall. The bullets and buckshot were viewed under a high intensity microscope. Tiny strands were found on the projectiles. Seems to be a metal alloy combined with a cloth they haven't yet completely identified. It appears similar to silk, but the composition is more durable and the fibers bound closer together. The metal fibers used included titanium and rhodium.''

"Rhodium was part of the bullet composition, too,'' Bolan noted. ''That's unusual, to say the least.''

"I hate to sound like the most ignorant guy in two rooms,'' Turrin said, ''but I've got to admit I don't even know what the hell rhodium is.''

"It's a hard, white element generally found in platinum ores,'' Kissinger explained. ''Needless to say, it isn't common. It's highly resistant to acids and other types of damage. Probably best known as an ingredient with platinum alloys, it helps make jewelry more durable because it doesn't scratch easily.''

"If it was used in that body armor, it would hold up pretty well under some extreme stress conditions,'' Bolan remarked. "Any idea who might have developed a type of body armor with a weave combination like that?''

"The Bear is working on it,'' Brognola answered. "No luck so far, but you know Aaron. He'll check every possibility every which way he can.''

"Yeah,'' Kissinger said, "he even came up with the source of the cocaine found at the crack house in L.A.''

"What's this?'' Bolan asked with surprise.

Brognola shuffled through some papers on the table, found the one he wanted and referred to it as he spoke.

"Aaron tapped into the mainframe of a DEA lab assigned to analyze the drugs and related paraphernalia. It turns out the composition of the cocaine fits a medium-quality grade known to be processed by a jungle-lab chemist they refer to as Dr. Petrol who works for a subfamily of El Dorado.''

"El Dorado,'' Bolan said with a frown of concentration. "That's a Bolivian syndicate, right?''

"Yep,'' the big Fed confirmed. "Dr. Petrol got his nickname because traces of gasoline were found in cocaine processed by the guy. They generally use kerosene to soak the coca leaves in the early stages of breaking cocaine down to the white powder. Dr. Petrol must have more access to gasoline, or maybe it's cheaper in the areas he operates from. For whatever reason, he uses gasoline instead of kerosene. The DEA says the guy's actually a pretty good chemist to turn out the quality of coke he's known for despite this practice. I don't know if this information will help us, but it seems worth mentioning.''

"Will it help much if we know the coke came from Bolivia instead of Colombia, Brazil or wherever they harvest coca leaves these days?'' Turrin asked. "It might be sort of interesting if the stuff was a product of this Dr. Petrol, but I don't know if that's useful, either.''

"It could be,'' Bolan said. "The armored men took the coke as well as the cash from the crack house. They must have taken it for a reason. I doubt they'll destroy it and it would be a hell of a lot for personal use, unless these guys have a taste for nose candy that could burn out the sinus passages of an army. Most likely they plan to sell the stuff themselves. If coke or crack cocaine processed by Dr. Petrol is identified at a location not known to carry his products before, it could help lead us to the enemy.''

"I don't think we can spend much more time and manpower on this project, Striker,'' Brognola said. "It doesn't qualify as a threat to national security at this time, and I doubt the President will approve our continuing with this, based on what we have so far.''

"Then the President will be making a mistake,'' Bolan said. "This is just the beginning, Hal. Whoever these people are, they won't stop now. They might have raked in more than two million dollars in cash and drugs with these two raids, but I wouldn't be surprised if each of those armored suits cost close to a million to make. They must have a larger objective than just ripping off bank robbers and drug dealers.''

"You may be right, Striker," Brognola admitted. "Do you have any idea what that might be?"

"Not yet, but they must want something big. They have established an organization that can effectively strike at different locations thousands of miles apart. Their members are well-trained in escape and evasion, as well as special combat skills. Even with the advanced protective gear, they have to be extremely motivated to carry out such bold and dangerous attacks. They also must have a pretty sophisticated Intelligence network to be able to select their targets. They've put all this together because they want something, and they'll keep going until they achieve their goal, or somebody stops them."

"Then we won't have long to wait before they show up again," Kissinger commented dryly.

He took a sheet of paper from the table and studied it. It was a copy of the pencil sketch Bolan had done of the armored gunman. The Cowboy looked at the drawing and whistled softly.

"This is one hell of an opponent," he said. "You hit these bastards point-blank in the breastplate and helmet without any effect. And the only target that was successful was the metal knee guard. That and the elbow guard are probably the closest things to weak spots on the body armor. The folds at these joints must be thinner than the rest of the suit to allow the wearer to bend his elbows and knees. Not very big targets to aim for."

"That shouldn't be a problem for Striker if he comes up against these killers again," Brognola said.

"Not since you gave him that special armor-piercing Parabellum ammo. Right, John?"

"I sure hope so," Kissinger replied.

"What's that supposed to mean?" the big Fed asked.

"It means the ammo I gave him is damn fine quality and ought to punch through just about any type of bulletproof vest, flak jacket or heavy protective gear. But I don't know if it'll pierce the outfits these guys have or not."

"You seemed confident it would work when you gave me the ammunition at the Farm this morning," Bolan reminded him.

"I was, but that was before I came back from the FBI labs and learned more about the body armor they're wearing. To be honest, I'm not so sure now. Better try to be careful if you run into them again."

"Yeah," Bolan replied, "I will."

6

Raymond Stylles had felt a surge of exhilaration when he'd put on the body armor. The suit was power, transforming him into an indestructible superman— the shell protecting him from harm, the helmet and visor concealing his identity. He rode in the back of the van, the special 10 mm submachine gun held on his lap. He was sure he could bring down a California redwood by blasting two magazines of the armor-piercing ammo into the base of the trunk.

Stylles had always dreamed of being feared and powerful. As a boy he had endured abuse from his father. He'd become a school-yard bully to rule over others, but he'd learned that was a mistake. Teachers reported his misconduct to his father, and the old man demonstrated his outrage with a belt.

Parents and teachers held authority over children, the boy had realized, so a position of authority gave one more power than just using one's fists. He'd applied himself in class with new determination, surprising everyone with his intellectual prowess. But still he'd remained angry and bitter, searching for some way to gain power and authority in a world that seemed to render him helpless.

The police had a form of authority that had appealed to the young Stylles. They carried clubs and guns, drove fast cars and arrested people who broke laws. Even those who didn't admire or respect the police feared them. He'd decided he wanted to be a cop. When he graduated from high school, he decided to enlist instead. The Army would train him to be a military policeman, and he would be sent far away from his father and the hometown he hated.

The military gave new life to Stylles. The physical and mental demands of his training were difficult, but he excelled in every task and subject. Private Stylles found the code of conduct that required respect for officers and NCOs harder to deal with, but he concealed his resentment and obeyed orders, as expected of a good soldier. When he realized one could achieve power and authority within the service, but that it would take years to achieve a high rank that would only apply within the military, he left with an honorable discharge and joined a civilian police department. He used the GI Bill to take college courses, before moving on to the FBI. If a cop had authority, he reasoned, a cop with the federal government had even more. However, he was once again disappointed by the amount of power this granted him and the long path required to rise through the ranks to achieve the position he desired.

As Stylles looked around at his four armor-clad companions, he knew this was the power he had dreamed of, the power to destroy all that stood in their way, to take what they wanted and crush any opposition. Gallow had called them Juggernauts, and Stylles felt like a god. Better, he *commanded* a group of warrior gods. It was power and authority beyond the grasp of mortal man.

It was almost enough for Raymond Stylles.

The van traveled north from the Loop on John F. Kennedy Expressway, then took an exit onto Lincoln Avenue and approached Albany Park. The vehicle came to a halt, and the driver turned to the five armored figures in the back.

"We're here," he announced. "I can suit up and ram the car that's parked in the driveway."

Stylles and the others in the back of the rig weren't able to see anything beyond the steel plates welded to the van's interior. "Is the front gate open or closed?" he asked the driver.

"Open. There are a couple of big guys by the car. They look like muscle boys."

"We can taken care of this," Stylles stated. "We don't want to get any dents or bullet holes in this van if we don't have to. There's no point in drawing the attention of the Chicago police if that stakeout team calls the cops."

"Are you sure that stakeout team is in this area?" one of his teammates inquired.

"It's there," Stylles assured him. "Let's hope they have enough sense to stay out of this. If not, we'll have to do whatever's necessary to complete tonight's mission."

He rose from the bench and opened the back door, emerging onto the pavement. He inspected the quiet, dark street in what would be called a good neighborhood: expensive housing away from the heavy traffic and noise at the heart of the city, a low crime area, populated by respectable citizens with sizeable incomes.

Stylles couldn't feel the breeze inside his body armor, but he saw the trees swaying, and clouds concealed the moon. He peered around the side of the vehicle and saw their objective.

A big, well-lit two-story house of brown brick with white trim stood in the center of a manicured lawn, surrounded by an ornate fence inset with iron gates. A lime green Mustang was parked in the drive, two goons in pin-stripe suits standing beside it, their faces turned toward the Juggernauts' van.

They probably thought it was a surveillance vehicle, Stylles mused, as if federal agents or narcs would be as obvious and careless as those stooges. Stylles had read the data on the immigrant gangsters, yet he could still hardly believe they advertised their activities in such a blatant manner. The pair looked like they were going to a costume party dressed as James Cagney and George Raft. But they weren't too funny to be involved in real crime with real imported merchandise about to go on the street market. The clowns in the pin-stripes also carried real guns, loaded with live ammunition.

So what? Stylles thought with a smile concealed by the tinted visor.

He stepped from the van and approached the house. He was careful not to move too quickly. The body armor was constructed of supertough alloys that weighed less than one might think for such formidable protection. Yet it was still heavy enough to wear out a man if he rushed about too much. Stylles and the other Juggernauts had trained for months in the armor and appreciated its restrictions as well as its strengths.

The two hoods at the gate stared, frozen, at the unearthly figure that marched toward the property. Stylles walked to the mouth of the gate, his gloved hand on the frame of the subgun that hung from a shoulder strap.

One of the thugs said something in a foreign language that Stylles didn't understand, nor did he care. He raised the barrel of the subgun and squeezed the trigger. A 3-round burst snarled from the muzzle, hurling the hood backward.

The other sentry yelled and yanked a pistol from his jacket. The Juggernaut turned to face him. He didn't bother to point his weapon at the gunman, but smiled as the thug opened fire. A bullet struck Stylles's breastplate, and he felt as if a finger had poked him in the chest. The enemy rapidly squeezed off two more shots, his face a mask of disbelief.

Stylles edged closer, then swung his gun arm. The heavy barrel slammed into the goon's extended arm, striking the pistol from his grasp. Stylles stepped forward, this time leading with his left foot and left fist. Steel spikes ripped flesh and the force of the punch splintered bone, as the thug was propelled into the side of the Mustang. Blood oozed from the gouges in the side of his face, his jawbone broken.

No heavyweight boxer could equal the destructive power of that left hook, Stylles thought with satisfaction. He grabbed the subgun in both gloved hands, driving the muzzle into his dazed opponent's abdomen. The man's body folded, and he fell face-first to the ground. Stylles raised a boot, then brought it down hard on the back of the fallen man's neck. The rubber sole of the boot covered a steel plate, and the Juggernaut's deadly stomp crushed vertebrae as if killing a cockroach.

Gunfire erupted from the house. Weapons blazed from the front entrance and at least one window, bullets ricocheting off Stylles's armor. The other Juggernauts entered the battle, returning fire with their subguns, shattering glass and gouging chunks of brick from the walls. A body tumbled from the threshold down the stone steps.

The door slammed shut as the five Juggernauts approached, Stylles assuming the lead as they marched up the steps. Pistols barked from an upstairs window, a bullet whining off Stylles's helmet. One of his companions raised his 10 mm subgun to respond with a 3-round burst. The lead Juggernaut ignored the fire as he stepped up to the door and launched a straight punch under the knob.

The blow struck like a battering ram. The bolt burst through the wood frame, and the door crashed open. Stylles walked inside to discover two opponents, their shotguns ready. As twin sprays of buckshot bounced off the Juggernaut raiders, Stylles fired his weapon from the hip. An enemy gunman went down, crashing onto the tiled floor. The second shotgunner jacked the slide of his 12-gauge, but one of the intruders blasted him with another trio of 10 mm slugs before he could bring his weapon into play.

Stylles looked about, turning his head from side to side within the helmet. They stood in a hallway, from which a staircase extended to the second story. One corridor led to a dining room, while the hallway opened into the living room.

"Some of them ran upstairs," Stylles declared loudly, compensating for the muffling effect of the helmets. "One of you stays here in case any of these idiots decide to come down, two of you guard the corridor and one man comes with me. You all know what we're looking for. If anybody gets in the way, terminate. There's no time to waste. We need to get out of here before the area is crawling with cops and Feds."

"That'll be their tough luck if they try to stop us," a Juggernaut replied.

"We're not here to kill law enforcement personnel," Stylles snapped. "We may have to, but only if it's necessary. Now move!"

The Juggernauts followed his instructions, two heading for the dining room, one remaining by the stairs, the other trailing Stylles through the living room. They approached the entrance to another room. Stylles recalled the information they'd gathered in preparation for the raid: the federal agents had focused their surveillance on an office on the first floor adjacent to the front room.

"I think we found the brass ring," Stylles remarked.

Another beefy thug reared in the doorway, an Ingram MAC-10 in his fists. He triggered the compact blaster, hitting the two Juggernauts with a furious volley of 9 mm Parabellum rounds. Stylles winced involuntarily when a slug struck his visor, level with his left eye, but the hard plastic held fast.

The gunman suddenly cried out and staggered

backward, his weapon rising with the fierce recoil and firing the last few rounds of the magazine into the ceiling. He stared at the blossoming red stain on his shirt, the expression on his broad Slavic face more one of surprise than pain.

"You were hit by one of your own bullets ricocheting off us, you moron," Stylles stated, supplying the answer to the gunner's unspoken question.

The thug bared his teeth as he hurled his empty weapon at them. It struck a Juggernaut's breastplate and bounced off it with even less effect than the bullets. Desperately the hardman lunged for Stylles, his fingers curved into claws as if he would tear the armor from the Juggernaut's body.

Stylles allowed the man to charge forward. As the thug grabbed the metal skin with both hands, Stylles slammed the crown of his helmet into his skull. The man staggered, blood dripping from his forehead. Anxious not to waste any more time, Stylles jammed the muzzle of his subgun into the man's chest, shooting him through the heart.

"*Nyet! Nyet!*" a voice cried from the office. "Do not shoot!"

Two men stood behind a large oak desk. Stylles recognized the round, middle-aged man from a photo fax. The would-be crime czar was sweating profusely into the collar of his expensive Italian suit.

Stylles didn't know who the scrawny character with the fat man might be, but he guessed he was the owner of the Mustang parked in the drive.

A mound of plastic bags containing white powder covered the desktop, and an empty suitcase sat on the floor next to a closed briefcase.

The fat man nervously cleared his throat and began to speak in halting English. "I do not know who you are, but we make a deal? Okay? You want money? I give you money. Plenty money—"

"Let's see it," Stylles demanded. "Make it quick, asshole."

"There is one hundred and fifty thousand dollars in that case," the fat man said, pointing to the attaché case.

Stylles guessed that was the payoff for delivering the dope. Rat-boy had brought the narcotics, intending to collect his money and leave as fast as possible. That explained why the gate had been left open and the Mustang parked in the driveway.

"A hundred and fifty grand is nothing," Stylles's companion complained. "Where's your safe?"

"I open it!" the mobster replied. "Do not worry."

"Just do it!" Stylles said, his weapon poised. "And your friend can pack that heroin back in the suitcase, as well."

The fat man moved to a liquor cabinet, removed some bottles and began to work the combination to a wall safe. The dealer started to stuff the plastic sacks into the suitcase, as gunfire continued to echo outside the room. Wailing sirens could be heard in the distance.

"Jesus," Rat-man rasped. "The cops are going to nail all of us! I've met some crazies, but you guys take the cake."

"Just shut up and do as you're told!" Stylles warned.

The mobster began to pile several stacks of bills

on the desk. Stylles knew that based on the street value of the drug, they were netting a sizeable haul.

"Get a bag or something for that money," Stylles ordered. "How do you think we're supposed to carry it?"

"I am sorry," the fat man stuttered, producing a small duffel bag. He hastily crammed the cash into it, while darting nervous glances at the two Juggernauts. Stylles casually raised his subgun and pointed it at the man's face. The other armored raider did the same to Rat-man.

Without a word, they opened fire in unison.

RAYMOND STYLLES and his henchman returned to the hall, burdened by the cases and bag. Corpses littered the area. The three Juggernauts assigned to deal with the opponents in the rest of the house waited there for Stylles and his assistant. None had been harmed during the battle, but flashing lights from outside warned them that they had another problem.

Stylles edged to the door. Police cars and at least two unmarked vehicles were positioned just beyond the gate.

"Damn," he muttered. "I didn't want it to come to this."

A voice bellowed through a bullhorn. "This is the FBI! We're here with the Chicago police and we have the house surrounded. A SWAT team is in place, and there's no way you can escape. Throw down your weapons and come out with your hands over your heads."

"That'll be the day," the Juggernaut leader growled, opening a pouch on his belt and removing a grenade. He turned to his men, ordering two of them to get their grenades ready, the other pair to open fire.

The Juggernauts charged from the house, submachine guns leading. Two uniformed policemen went down immediately. An FBI agent ducked for cover behind the open door of his unmarked car, but three 10 mm slugs drilled through the barrier, getting him in the chest.

Law-enforcement weapons roared in reply, bullets and shotgun pellets slamming the Juggernauts' body armor from all directions. Stylles couldn't raise his arm to lob the grenade because so many projectiles pounded his limbs and shoulders, but he managed to toss the bomb underhand. It rolled between two police cars and exploded, sending fiery wreckage and ravaged human forms hurtling across the street.

Stylles grabbed his weapon, adding to the raking gunfire, while another Juggernaut threw the second grenade.

More vehicles exploded. A river of flaming gasoline began to flow among the police and federal agents, sending burning figures fleeing. Suddenly a heavy-caliber slug smashed onto Stylles's helmet. It was from a SWAT sniper, he guessed, as the projectile was followed by a tear gas canister. It landed near the Juggernauts, but their helmets and armor shielded them from the immediate effects of the CS gas.

Stylles led his troops past the gate as the third grenade targeted another cluster of police vehicles. The explosion erupted around them as the Juggernauts reached the street. A patrolman bravely opened fire with a shotgun. His buckshot bounced off a breastplate and a 3-round dose of 10 mm slugs pitched him across the pavement. Snipers continued to try to stop the gray figures, but their accurate head shots only caused the Juggernauts' helmeted heads to jerk on impact. The formerly heavy salvo of gunfire had been drastically reduced, and the Juggernauts made steady progress toward their van.

A SWAT officer appeared at the mouth of an alley, M-16 assault rifle to his shoulder. He hit Stylles with a burst of 5.56 mm projectiles. The Juggernaut commander spotted the black-clad cop by the muzzle-flashes from his assault rifle. Returning fire with his subgun, he drilled the SWAT commando, dropping him in the alley.

The Juggernauts moved on. A wounded policeman lay in their path. He tried to crawl from them, but his leg had been smashed by an armor-piercing round through the thigh. The man had lost his weapon and Stylles was content to walk around the unarmed man, but another Juggernaut had less mercy. He kicked the cop in the face with the steel toe of his boot, knocking him unconscious, blood streaming from his mouth. The last Juggernaut in the group paused to stomp on the helpless figure, his reinforced boot carving in the officer's chest.

"And this little piggy went to hell!" the murderer declared, chuckling.

Darkness had vanished, replaced by the light generated by burning gasoline and debris. Gunfire had ceased. Even the snipers had stopped shooting, allowing the Juggernauts to reach their vehicle. Stylles saw the startled face of their driver. He stared at the street, clearly stunned by the horrific spectacle before him.

"Start the engine, damn it!" Stylles ordered. "We've got to get out of here!"

"Holy shit!" the driver exclaimed. "I don't believe it, man. You must've killed a hundred cops—"

"Just shut up and do your job!" the Juggernaut replied.

The armored men climbed into the back of the rig. As Stylles placed the suitcase on the metal floor, he noticed white powder leaking from several holes in the container. The damn cops had hit the suitcase. He cursed, wondering how much of their profits had been spilled onto the street when he saw that the duffel bag and briefcase had also been riddled by bullets.

He slammed the door, and the van screamed away from the curb. They would ditch the rig as planned and move on in other vehicles. Police roadblocks would soon be set up, if they weren't already in position. They needed to get as far away as possible in a very short time.

"That's one hell of a mess you left back there," the driver said.

"Yeah, but we got what we wanted," Stylles replied.

7

Yellow police tape sealed off what the police referred to as the crime scene, but to the Executioner, it resembled a combat zone. The charred remains of vehicles and bodies littered the streets, and the stench of burned rubber and the sickly sweet scent of roasted human flesh still hung in the air.

"You could have told me this place was bombed from the air and I'd figure it was true," Leo Turrin said. "These bastards are getting kill crazy, Mack."

"I think they already were," Bolan replied, watching the FBI investigator in charge and the Chicago PD liaison officer talk with a member of the federal forensics unit and a couple other men in the single-breasted suits Turrin called "Fed uniforms."

Albert Monroe, the Bureau investigator, approached Bolan and Turrin. A stocky African-American, he looked as if he carried an invisible fifty-pound burden of responsibility on his back, and stress lines were etched deeply into his face.

"You guys from Justice got here pretty quick," he commented. "I hear you were already working on something similar on the West Coast."

"Yeah," Turrin answered, "but it wasn't as bad as this."

"I can't imagine it gets much worse than this," the FBI agent replied. "There were forty-seven federal agents and Chicago police in this area. Now we got eighteen dead and twenty-one in the hospital, and some of them might not pull through. That's not including all the dead hoods they carried out of that house. I think tonight kicked up the Chicago homicide rate to put it in competition with D.C. for the year. Murder statistics are going to look like a telephone number, complete with area code."

"We know the Bureau had this house under surveillance," Bolan said, "but we're not quite sure who these people were or why you had them staked out."

"We won't have to worry about them anymore," Monroe said as he handed a clipboard to Turrin. "Most of them are dead, with only a couple of low-life underlings left of the gang."

Turrin glanced at the names of identified bodies taken from the house. He blinked with surprise.

"You got to be kidding," he said. "Capone, Nitti, Luciano... These guys were pulled out of here tonight?"

"Isn't that too much?" Monroe said, with something that could have been a smile with a little more effort. "These jokers actually changed their names after they came to the U.S. Vito Capone even went to court to legally change his name from Dimitri Ivanovich Zhukov."

"So they were Russian immigrants," Bolan commented. "There's been a big increase in organized crime in Russia since the fall of the Soviet Union, and the syndicates have branched out to other countries, including America."

"Yeah," Monroe confirmed, "but these clowns were more 'disorganized' crime. Zhukov and his boys weren't exactly ex-KGB master spies turned brilliant gangster warlords."

"Not when they make mistakes this stupid," Turrin said. "They even picked names that made them suspicious."

"That's how we first suspected they were up to something crooked," the FBI man said. "It didn't take any great insight to make that assumption. These Russians wanted to be some sort of self-styled Italian-American Mafia Family, and they were obvious about it."

"How did these aspiring capitalists plan to make their fortune?" Bolan asked.

"What's someone's choice to make big bucks in a big hurry?" Monroe said. "Drugs, of course. At first it was difficult to take these guys seriously. The stakeout team had a bug planted in the house, and these guys were listening to the soundtrack from *The Godfather* every night like it was inspirational music. But then they actually started to make some big money. It turns out they managed to get a connection with some smugglers working out of Montrose Harbor over by Wrigley Field. They were expecting a shipment of heroin to arrive. Although we still sort of doubted it, the Chicago cops and the DEA agreed to stand by, just in case. Then it came down tonight. Nobody expected what else was going to happen."

"The men in body armor," Bolan stated.

"The bastards just showed up," the FBI agent said. "They marched right through the gate, blowing away anybody who got in their way. When they came out there was a small army of cops and Feds, dug in and ready for trouble. SWAT was set up with enough firepower to bring down a couple of hundred armed felons. They were prepared to take on about two dozen Russian gunmen, and instead they came up against five guys in armored suits and helmets. Just five guys!''

"Five bulletproofed opponents armed with powerful armor-piercing weapons," Bolan amended. "You couldn't have expected that, or been prepared for them. Believe me, I understand."

"Right, you've seen these bastards before," Monroe said. "So, who the hell are they? How long have they been pulling this sort of crap?"

"We know about them," Turrin replied, "but we still don't have any idea who they are, where they come from or why they're doing this."

"Well," the agent said, "I think it's safe to assume they wanted money and dope. They cleaned out Capone's safe before they blew his brains. Survivors from the shoot-out said they were carrying baggage of some kind. Bullets must have punctured the bag with the heroin. They left a trail of white powder from here to their getaway vehicle. DEA swept it up and they're having it analyzed, whatever good that'll do."

"You never know what might help," Bolan said. "Did you get a videotape of the incident?"

"The stakeout team across the street got it on tape. The Chicago PD and DEA had cameras, too, but those were destroyed when the bastards started throwing grenades. What the hell were those guys wearing? Two SWAT sharpshooters were posted on rooftops with a couple of those NATO sniper rifles. They swear they nailed direct hits to the heads of those killers, but they couldn't bring them down. A couple of guys think they might be some sort of killer robots developed by the government that have gone out of control.''

"Afraid not,'' Bolan told him. "It's worse than that.''

MACK BOLAN STRETCHED in a series of warm-up exercises, while Leo Turrin set up the laptop computer on the desk.

"I've got the Farm on-line,'' he announced as he punched in the access code.

Bolan crossed the room to join Turrin as Hal Brognola appeared on the screen. The Stony Man chief had a stack of files in front of him and a cigar butt in his hand.

"How do you guys like Chicago?'' he asked.

"We haven't seen much of it this trip,'' Bolan answered. "Just the site of the most recent attack by the body-armor killers and our motel.''

"I understand it was pretty bad.''

"Yeah, but this time they got a videotape of the attackers. It might help Cowboy make some evaluations about the body armor if he gets to see it being worn in action.''

"You won't need to broadcast the tape,'' Brognola said. "Aaron already got a copy via his computer link with the FBI. The damn thing will probably hit the regular TV news within the next six hours or so. Reports about a big gun battle between mystery men in armor and helmets and Russian mobsters don't remain secret.''

"Do any of the reports mention that all the law-enforcement officers killed or injured were struck down by the guys in body armor, not the Russians?" Turrin asked.

"Early reports haven't made that clear. The good news is that I think we'll be able to get the President to support continued work on this assignment, so consider it an official mission at this point, Striker. The President will certainly see this as a national concern when he learns so many police and federal agents have fallen victim to these killers. We can't dismiss this as the work of a small gang of vigilantes."

"Any good news is welcomed," Bolan assured him. "We could also use any news that would help us guess where these murderers will show up next. They're damn sure busy and bold. Only a few days have passed since they first struck in Pittsburgh. These people aren't stupid. They must have good reason to accept the risks of being so active in such a short period of time."

"Maybe they plan to rake in as big a profit as possible from cash and drugs before they vanish. As nobody knows who they are, they could just shed their armor and head for Rio."

"That's possible, Hal," the Executioner allowed, "but I doubt it. That body armor and other gear must have taken a long time and considerable expense to develop. I don't think that was done just to rob a bunch of hoods. I still think they want more than that."

Brognola reached for a file and glanced over it as he spoke. "This is an update on that FBI lab investigation of fibers found on the bullets in Pittsburgh.

You remember they identified titanium and rhodium among the alloys, along with something similar to silk. That something turned out to be spiderweb strands.''

"Spiderweb?'' Turrin repeated.

"Yeah,'' Brognola confirmed, checking his data. "From one of the largest of a type commonly called fishing spiders. It says here that these spiders actually catch small fish and tadpoles. Can you imagine a spider doing that?''

"I can't imagine one spinning a bulletproof vest,'' Turrin replied. "You sure these guys at the FBI aren't sniffing glue in that lab?''

"Actually there's been research into using woven spiderweb strands for that purpose for some years now, according to this report,'' the big Fed went on. "It's believed that spiderweb could be stronger than Kevlar, if compressed and weaved in the correct manner.''

"So, somebody combined a weave of the spider strands with the metal alloy fibers to construct the body armor,'' Bolan mused. "They must have come up with that idea after a lot of trial and error. Whoever developed it might have worked on similar projects for the military or police at one time.''

"We're considering that possibility,'' Brognola assured him. "Aaron is doing a computer scan on personnel who might fit that profile. He's been busting his tail as usual. He also came across information about some cocaine that showed up in Detroit. You remember that business about Dr. Petrol, the jungle chemist who uses gasoline in processing his coke?

Well, the coke in Detroit might have come from the L.A. supply taken by the body-armor troopers.''

"How did this show up in Detroit?" Bolan asked.

"A street pusher tried to sell the stuff to an undercover narc. I'll fax you the information if you think it's worth looking into."

"It might be a lead," the Executioner said. "Leo is better at dealing with federal investigators and agencies than I am. Cowboy is qualified to handle the data concerning body armor and ballistics. I might go to Detroit and see if there's a connection, unless something else occurs that seems more promising."

"I hope something pans out pretty soon," Brognola said. "These killers haven't been letting much time pass between hits, and each seems more brutal than the last. The body count keeps rising and it's including a lot of good guys, as well as bank robbers and drug dealers."

"We'll stop the body count from rising when we stop the enemy," Bolan replied. "Let's just hope we find them before they strike again."

8

Malachi Jones frowned as he studied the stock exchange listings in the *Wall Street Journal*. Commodities were down again. His shares in major computer and telecommunications companies had also dropped in value. How had that happened? Modern technology was supposed to be the way of the future, yet his stock was taking a nosedive.

"What's with this economy?" he grumbled. "We got a recession or an inflation, or what?"

"I just put money in T-bills and a couple of IRAs," Stanley, Jones's bodyguard, remarked. "I figure it's better to save and let interest build than to try to make any big profits with the market the way it is."

"You don't make any money that way," Jones said. "And somebody's making money out there, Stanley. Whenever the economy makes a huge shift one way or the other, you can bet some damn insiders are making a profit somehow."

"You're probably right, Mr. Malachi."

"Damn right I am. I just have to figure out what those guys are doing and get into it myself."

Stanley nodded, not daring to get into an argument with his boss.

No one called Malachi Jones "Mr. Jones." It seemed too common for such an uncommon man.

Jones had come a long way from his first job as a young mule in Detroit's drug trade, which led to a position as a dealer at his high school. He was proud of the fact that he'd graduated and even spent two years at Michigan State College studying business and economics. The knowledge he'd gained had helped his career in the sale and distribution of narcotics.

He liked to consider himself a successful African-American businessman, using the drug trade to get ahead, until he could retire from it and move into a respectable legal business. Perhaps he would even start a scholarship for young blacks interested in business law and economics. Unfortunately he had more success coordinating his small syndicate of dealers and mules than investing in legitimate enterprise.

Jones put down the paper and sipped some coffee from a small china cup. His morning hadn't started very well: bad news on the stock exchange, and soon he expected a visitor connected with other bad news he had received earlier. He ignored his eggs and hash browns, his appetite affected by his woes, instead finishing his coffee as he looked at his bodyguard. A former professional athlete, Stanley had been a promising ball player with the Tigers before he'd served time for manslaughter. Jones had recognized potential in Stanley. Bright, tough and disciplined both mentally and physically, the man proved to be a splendid combination of adviser, bodyguard and manservant.

"I need to estimate how serious my losses have

been,'' Jones said, ''and how I can recover a profit by some other avenue of income.''

''I don't know about the stock market,'' Stanley muttered. ''I figure those white boys on Wall Street have that sucker tied up for themselves.''

''Nonsense. My money is just as green as theirs. They didn't downgrade stocks and commodities just to hurt me financially. I made some bad choices. It worked out on paper, but it went sour in actual practice. Every businessman has to accept a few losses. It's part of the game.''

The doorbell rang. Stanley took a checkered red vest from a coat rack and put it on as he headed for the door, the vest concealing his holstered snub-nosed .357 Magnum revolver. In his opinion, such early visitors showed a lack of consideration, and he knew Mr. Malachi didn't like discussing business while still wearing his robe and slippers.

Stanley returned with the visitor, a slender young man, whose eyes were fixed on his feet as he walked. His footgear was the most expensive item of clothing the young man wore. A denim jacket, blue jeans with rips at the knees and a felt hat with a wide brim made a fashion statement that caused Jones to grunt with disapproval.

''You look like the shabbiest pimp in Detroit, Ron,'' the dealer remarked. ''You should be embarrassed.''

''I am, Mr. Malachi,'' Ron Wayton replied. ''I would have changed, but I knew you wanted to see me right away.''

''Actually I wanted you here at 11:00 a.m. You're very early.''

"I'm sorry. Do you want me to come back later?"

"You're here now, so let's get this over with. And take off that stupid hat!"

Wayton snatched the offending article from his head and clutched it in front of him. He hadn't been invited to sit, so he remained on his feet. Stanley stepped up behind him. Wayton seemed nervous, aware that the bodyguard packed heat.

"The other day I gave you some cocaine to sell," Jones began. "I also gave you instructions to only sell the merchandise to persons you had done business with in the past. Do you recall that, Ron?"

"Yes, sir, Mr. Malachi."

"Then why did you attempt to sell the coke to someone you didn't know, someone who proved to be an undercover narc?"

"He didn't look like a narc," Wayton said lamely.

Jones raised his eyebrows. "That's strange, because he *was* a narc. Since you obviously can't recognize a cop in plainclothes, you should have followed my orders and dealt only with known customers."

"The dude was in a big limo. He looked like a high roller. Who would have thought a cop would be riding around in a limo?"

"I would have suspected that, Ron. The fact is, you didn't do what I told you to do and that's going to cost me a lot of money. Providing you with a lawyer and bail was just part of it."

"I'm real thankful to you for doing that."

"Don't be too thankful because I want you to know I'm unhappy with your conduct, and it's going to cost you. Any idea how much that should be, Ron? How about you, Stanley?''

The bodyguard took that as his cue, slamming a hard fist into Wayton's kidney. The street dealer groaned and staggered forward. He caught the edge of the table with one hand as the other plunged into his pocket, emerging with a switchblade knife, his thumb on the button.

''You know better than that, Ron,'' Jones warned.

Reluctantly Wayton put away the knife. He glared at Stanley, the bodyguard's face a mask.

Jones poured himself another cup of coffee. ''The lawyer's fee and bail money will be extracted from your pay until the debt has been covered. You had just better hope it doesn't go to court, because your costs will be higher. The lawyer believes he can claim entrapment by getting supportive testimony that police, disguised as wealthy customers, cruised the area asking how they could purchase some high-quality cocaine. You have a record as a user, Ron, but not a dealer. We'll say this was your first time attempting to sell dope in a desperate effort to support your own habit. There's a good chance we can get you off the hook by having you finger someone else as your supplier. The cops will probably drop charges against you to go after bigger fish.''

''That sounds good, Mr. Malachi.''

''It's better than you deserve, but I don't want my people going to jail. It's not good for our image. I'll probably have to take you off the street, and that means the cocaine will take longer to move and thus my profits will take longer to come in. That doesn't make me happy, Ron.''

He nodded at his bodyguard, who suddenly hooked his left fist under Wayton's ribs, driving the wind from the young man's lungs. Stanley grabbed the collar of Wayton's jacket with both hands and pumped a knee into the smaller man's groin. Wayton doubled up with a wheezing moan, then fell to the floor where Stanley gave him a final kick to the ribs.

"That's enough," Jones said. "I don't want him bleeding all over the carpet."

Wayton coughed, trying to get his breath as he rolled into a kneeling position.

"You know I don't enjoy these strong-arm tactics," Jones went on. "I simply can't have my people thinking they can disobey my orders, jeopardize my business transactions and slow down the distribution of my product. I want you to go home and stay there for now. We'll see what the lawyer can work out with the DA."

"I'll do like you say," Wayton replied. "That narc just looked like he'd be a big spender ready to buy a lot of coke."

"I'll have to figure which one of the local suppliers we'll accuse of giving you the coke to sell," Jones said, ignoring Wayton's excuses. "Maybe Rappo Rogers. I've always found him foolish, anyway. Speaking of which, I want you to get rid of that switchblade and any other illegal weapons. The cops may come to check on you. That means no guns, drugs, or anything else that can lead them to me. I'll be sending someone to make sure you have obeyed me, and things will go badly for you if they find anything."

"Sure, Mr. Malachi."

"If everything works out, I'll have to send you to another location, maybe Dearborn or Ann Arbor. I have some business deals in the works there."

"Ann Arbor?" Wayton asked as if the words tasted bad in his mouth. "I was born and raised here. Detroit is all I know. What kind of place is Ann Arbor for a guy like me?"

"Your life experience has been too restricted, Ron. Perhaps you need to grow more so you'll have a higher opinion of yourself and those you work for. You'll probably have to go back to being a mule for a while until I feel you can be trusted to deal again."

"A mule?" The street dealer seemed ready to protest, but then apparently thought better of the idea. "I guess it's better than going back to the joint."

"Or making a trip to the bottom of the river. This discussion is over. Show him to the door, Stanley."

Wayton got to his feet and limped to the door, accompanied by the bodyguard. As they exited, the telephone rang.

"Morning, Malachi." Raymond Stylles's voice came through the wire. "How's business?"

"Mr. Webster," Jones said, using the cover name favored by the man. "Nice to hear from you. Business has been promising, but there have been some setbacks. It's hard to get good help these days."

Stylles chuckled. "Well, I did give you good merchandise. You were certainly happy with the quality and the price."

"Absolutely, but let's not forget you needed the cash, so the deal seemed all right to you at the time."

"I didn't call to complain. The fact is, I might have some more goods for you if you'd like to make another investment. It has the potential to make a twenty-fold profit.''

"That does sound interesting. We should talk."

"I'll be in town later today. Is five o'clock good for you?"

"Make it six. We'll have dinner at the Lake Bistro."

"Fine. I think you'll like this offer, Malachi."

"That's the best news I've had all morning."

RON WAYTON DESCENDED the stairs to his basement apartment in a building on Kercheval Avenue. The neighborhood had gone from unsavory to bad during the two years he had lived there. Street gangs had gotten larger, better armed and even more crazy than when Wayton had been running with the Splinters.

That had been almost ten years earlier. Wayton had been a fifteen-year-old kid trying to be tough, smart and successful with money and women. The Splinters had led only to a stay in juvenile detention and a crack cocaine habit. Wayton had cut a few dudes in the joint, but he never really got a reputation as a tough guy. Nobody figured he was smart, and Wayton himself had no illusions in that regard. He played the streets as best he could, doing some fetch-and-carry jobs to support his romance with the glass-stemmed pipe.

Eventually he'd gotten a job with Mr. Malachi. The man was everything Wayton wanted to be. People genuinely respected him, and he had real class and dignity. Wayton did his best to please his master. He handled stolen merchandise for a year, carried dope as a mule for another eight or nine months, and finally earned the position of a crack pusher in the ghetto.

For Wayton, that was the pinnacle of his career. He'd tried to keep his intake of dope to a minimum, aware Mr. Malachi never really trusted anybody who sucked on a crack pipe. Wayton had hoped to one day earn a position as a big dealer, peddling pure coke and other drugs to upper-middle-class clients, but when Mr. Malachi had finally given him a chance to move some cocaine, he'd gone and blown it.

He unlocked the door to his apartment and entered, slamming the door shut and shoving the bolt home. A gasp of surprise rose from his throat when he saw the man by the bathroom doorway, a big white dude dressed in black. A bulge under his black jacket told Wayton the man packed some serious heat.

"Had a busy morning?" Mack Bolan inquired as he stepped forward.

"Who are—?"

"Why don't you just call me Favor because that's why I'm here. I'm looking for a favor, and I'll do you and your boss one in return."

Wayton narrowed his eyes. "This is a bad neighborhood for you to be hanging around in, white man, and this sure as hell ain't the right crib to be busting into."

"Are you afraid I'd lift that stash of crack and the pipe you've got wrapped in plastic in your toilet tank?"

"You're a cop," Wayton snapped. "You planted that dope on me. I'm calling my lawyer! This is harassment."

"I'm not a cop," Bolan replied. "If I was, I'd have

a search warrant and your landlord here to let me in legally. He would have seen me find your stash so I'd have a witness. I had no trouble finding it. It was the first place I looked. You junkies still think it's so smart to hide it in the toilet so you can flush it in a hurry.''

"I ain't saying nothing without my lawyer, pig.''

Bolan sighed and stepped closer. The apartment was a dump, littered with trash and discarded clothing. He didn't want to stay any longer than necessary.

"You've got a pretty expensive lawyer, Wayton. It doesn't look as if you could afford your bail money, let alone a high-priced attorney.''

"Arnold Collay offers special rates to minorities unduly victimized by society and a prejudiced legal system.''

"Arnold Collay won't even pick up his briefcase unless someone has already paid him at least five grand up front,'' Bolan replied. "He's represented so many big drug dealers that his list of clients looks like the DEA's most wanted. One of his clients is a man known as Malachi Jones.''

Wayton shoved both hands in his pockets and shrugged as he said, "Never heard of him, man.''

"Hell, you work for him. You were peddling his cocaine last night, a small part of a big shipment he received recently from a national distributor.''

The petty pusher stiffened, clearly startled by the statement. He thought for a moment before he spoke.

"You say you ain't a cop. That means you broke in here illegally. That's breaking and entering. I'm going to call the police and my lawyer.''

"You haven't noticed your phone is missing?'' Bolan asked. "I unplugged it from the wall jack and put it away. You're not going to call anyone, Wayton. You're taking me to Malachi Jones to discuss some business."

"I don't know nothing, so you'd better back off, honkie."

"My name's Favor, remember? We're going to help each other."

"Okay," Wayton said with a shrug. "If you put it that way—"

His hand suddenly emerged from his pocket and the blade snapped into view. He lunged, desperate to plunge the knife into the stranger before the man could go for his gun inside his jacket.

The Executioner responded immediately to the attack. His left hand swung into Wayton's forearm, deflecting the knife thrust. He moved with the swing, stepping beside his opponent, his right hand quickly snaring Wayton's wrist above the weapon. With his left hand he chopped into the crook of Wayton's elbow, forcing the arm to bend.

Jamming the dealer's bent elbow into the crook of his left arm, he grabbed the man's knife fist with both hands and pushed down. Bone popped as Wayton's wrist was abruptly bent more than the joint could handle. He cried out, the switchblade falling from his fingers.

Bolan released Wayton, who wailed in pain. Then his eyes widened with fear when he saw the stranger draw the Beretta 93-R pistol from his shoulder leather.

"Do I finally have your cooperation?" the Executioner asked.

"My wrist!" Wayton moaned. "You broke my wrist, you bastard!"

"Take me to Malachi Jones or you'll die right here and now."

"Mr. Malachi will kill me."

"Mr. Malachi isn't holding a gun to your head at this moment. I am," Bolan reminded him. "So, do you take me to him, or do I squeeze the trigger and find another way to meet your boss?"

"Mr. Malachi's not going to like this. We'll be lucky if he doesn't kill us both!"

"Let's see how our luck holds up," Bolan said.

Wayton shook his head, but he headed toward the door.

9

The President of the United States glanced over the speech he was scheduled to deliver to the graduating class at Cleveland State University that afternoon, as Air Force One descended below the clouds and circled Cleveland-Hopkins International Airport. It would soon land, and he'd have to carry out the usual ritual of waving at crowds and displaying a wide smile before getting into a car with a ring of Secret Service men around him. Then he'd be taken to the function that was more for public relations than of any substantial benefit to Ohioans.

The President's popularity had dropped in the polls, and his press secretary had urged him to make some public appearances across the nation in an effort to put him in the spotlight. The Man thought his time would be better spent in Washington, where the Senate debated two bills already passed by the House. The President opposed one and supported the other. And there was also the bizarre reports of armor-clad gunmen popping up all over the country, allegedly shooting down criminals and law-enforcement personnel. Hal Brognola of Stony Man Farm seemed convinced that it was a genuine threat to national security and the welfare of the country, but the President still had his doubts. He respected the Justice man's opinion, but he wasn't sure that a handful of men in body armor and helmets presented any real problems for the entire United States.

"Excuse me, Mr. President?"

He glanced up at Vince Kendall, unit chief of security for Air Force One. The man's expression seemed serious.

"What is it, Vince?"

"We got a call on a secure line to the mobile phone system. It's not exactly a hot line, but somebody had to get access to a satellite link in order to use it. It's a pretty sophisticated trick, and even finding out about the system isn't something your average hacker could manage."

"You mean somebody is on the phone who isn't supposed to have the number?" the President asked, his eyebrows knitted with concern.

"Essentially. The guy says he's the captain of the Juggernauts, supposedly connected with those characters running around in body armor and helmets."

"Oh, my God," the President said. "Is he on the line now?"

"Yes, sir. We tried to run a trace, but we can only track the signal to the telecommunications satellite he's using. It sounds like he has some sort of 'electronic handkerchief' that distorts the user's voice and even alters the pattern to a voice print to avoid identification when recording the call."

"Let me speak to him."

"That might not be a good idea, sir."

"I want to know what these people are up to, and

this is the most direct way to find out. Where's the phone unit?''

"I'll bring it to you. This is as secure a cabin as we've got here.''

Kendall left the President's quarters, returning shortly with a telecommunications device set in a metal attaché case. The Man picked up the handset.

"Hello, Mr. President.'' The man's voice was echoey, sounding as if it came from the bottom of a well. "How do you like Ohio? Ever eat one of those buckeyes? It sort of looks like a chestnut but tastes real bad.''

"I wouldn't know,'' the President replied. "Who are you, and what do you want?''

"You don't need to know my name yet. I represent the Juggernauts. That flunky I talked to before didn't explain that? He must have, or we wouldn't be talking now.''

"You people are thieves and murderers. I don't know how you got access to this line, but I don't do business with people like you.''

"Come now, Mr. President. You've had the heads of Third World dictatorships as guests of honor at the White House who have had thousands of people killed. We've killed some drug dealers and bank robbers. Does that really offend you more than having dinner with a savage in a tuxedo who stays in power by slaughtering anyone in his country who opposes him?''

"Save your twisted rationalizations for the psychiatrists your defense lawyer will call in to support your insanity plea when you go to trial. You Juggernauts,

as you call yourselves, have also killed numerous police officers and federal agents.''

"No, we didn't. They were killed by the bad
guys.''

"*You* are the bad guys. Ballistics reports confirmed
the same kind of armor-piercing bullets were used to
kill law-enforcement officers as those fired into the
criminals you admit you killed.''

"So you have taken an interest in our activities,''
the man said with a chuckle. "Those ballistics reports
are wrong. You'll have to get that straightened out
when you explain we were really assisting the police,
the FBI and the DEA. Unfortunately for them, they
don't have the same sort of advanced body armor and
weaponry we have. Of course, in the future there
won't be any need for law-enforcement personnel to
be harmed. Not after the Juggernauts become the pri-
mary force to restore law and order in the United
States.''

The President was stunned by that remark. He
didn't blurt out a response; words were a main part
of his professional life and he appreciated their value
more than most. He remained silent as he evaluated
the Juggernaut's statement.

"Are you still there, Mr. President?'' the Juggernaut inquired.

"I didn't know you had finished talking. You said
something about becoming the force for law and order. How do you plan to do that?''

"We're doing it already, surely you realize that.
We have established an Intelligence network that's
almost as efficient as any the federal agencies have in
place, even without the support and financial backing

they enjoy. Even with our limitations we've been able to locate nests of dangerous, ruthless criminals that prey on innocent citizens. We've dealt with these scum in the only way that works. We've done so because it was necessary.''

''It was necessary to kill all of them?''

''Please, Mr. President, we're not talking about traffic violations and shoplifting. These were heavily armed, violent criminals. They would have killed us if they could. Believe me, they tried. The local police and federal agencies knew about the hoodlum trash, but they didn't deal with it. We did.''

''The Pittsburgh police arrived at the bank robbers' hideout, and both local authorities and federal agents were at the site of those Russian gangsters in Chicago.''

''They just got in the way. Too bad about it, but it doesn't have to happen again. If we get your support and the support of those in government you can influence, then we won't have any problems with those outdated, poorly equipped and badly trained law personnel. We can do what they can't. We've already proved that, Mr. President. We are the Juggernauts. We are invincible and able to take out any opponent we encounter.''

''And you really think I'd agree to let you Juggernauts take the place of our local and federal law enforcement?''

''You might not be convinced yet,'' the man went on, ''but we are the only solution to this country's crime problem. Ask the people of this nation what their number-one concern is. Most will tell you they fear for their lives because of crime. Ask them if they mind that we had to kill some demented savage bank robbers who stole more than a million dollars and left a string of bodies in their wake. Ask them if they object that some drug dealers, who peddled poison to their children and collected money from junkies who support their habit by robbing innocent victims, are now dead. The public doesn't care how we get rid of such vermin. They just want us to do it.''

''The American people might not approve of your tactics as much as you seem to think they will.''

''Gangs are running wild in every major city in the U.S. They're armed with full-auto weapons and they don't give a damn who they kill. Innocent people, often children, are gunned down during drive-by shootings by these mad dogs. The police can't stop them, social workers can't reason with them, and even if you pass more laws, they'll just break them and continue to behave in this murderous manner. We can stop them. They can't shoot down the Juggernauts. Their weapons might be better than what the cops have, but they can't match our firepower and might.''

''So your answer to crime is to kill them all?''

''We'll be willing to arrest anyone smart enough to surrender to us. We obviously couldn't make citizens' arrests at the previous incidents. That will change when we're the official law-enforcement officers throughout the country.''

''If you intend, as you say, to enforce the law, why did you take money and drugs from those previous sites?''

''We don't have federal funding, so we have to finance our organization with what we can take from the enemy. Haven't money and property taken from criminals been used to fund the war on drugs? Speaking of which, the DEA has complained for years that the criminal syndicates are better financed and better armed than they are. The Juggernauts don't have limitless financial resources and our manpower is small, but we've already shown we're superior to the DEA or the drug syndicates. Imagine what we can do with adequate resources.''

''The mind boggles,'' the President muttered before he could stop himself. ''What did you do with the cocaine and heroin you got in Los Angeles and Chicago? A lot of those drugs were supposed to be at both sites.''

''Oh, we destroyed the drugs, of course. We couldn't leave that stuff lying around. Kids might have gotten into it.''

''We have to protect the children,'' the President said, deciding to play along with the man. ''Do you have any idea how much this proposal of yours might cost the taxpayers?''

''I don't think it would cause an increase in their tax burden if you have us replace police and federal agents dealing with the most serious crime situations. We Juggernauts can get more accomplished with fewer men. We must insist on picking our own people, though. Selection, training and conditioning will be up to us, and us only. It takes a special kind of man to be a Juggernaut.''

''I'm sure of that,'' the President replied, continuing the charade. ''It might take awhile to convince the House and Senate, or even my own cabinet, that we should fire thousands of law-enforcement personnel, and pretty much scrap the FBI, the DEA, Justice and whatever else, and let you guys run the show. I know the attorney general won't like it.''

"You don't seem to like the idea either, Mr. President. You probably think we're insane, don't you?"

"No. I didn't say anything to suggest that."

"Of course you didn't. Only a fool would tell a madman he's crazy. I didn't think you'd be ready to agree to this. Right now, you think you're dealing with some lunatics, and you're trying to get information you can pass on to the FBI or whomever to try to track us down. Don't bother to deny it, Mr. President."

"Anything I say won't satisfy you at this point. If I do talk to my advisers, they'll want to speak with you before they will even consider what you suggest."

"You think I'm going to give you a phone number? Don't be absurd. It's clear you'll need more proof that the Juggernauts can succeed at dealing with crime, but any efforts to stop us will only result in more tragedy for the families of the police and federal agents you claim you care about."

"Making threats isn't a good way to gain cooperation with the federal government."

"No one is making a threat," the voice insisted. "You simply have only one course of action, and you'll have to agree to it. You can expect to hear from us again in the near future. Actually you'll probably be hearing a great deal about us even sooner. Have a good time in Ohio, and remember to stay away from those buckeyes."

Suddenly the transmission ended, and the President returned the handset to the case. Kendall stared at him, uncertain what, if anything, he should say. The Man glanced at his wristwatch.

"Tell the pilot to circle the airport until I tell him to land," he said. "I need to contact someone about this Juggernaut business."

"We can arrange a conference call with the directors of the FBI and the National Security Agency if you wish to speak with them simultaneously," the security chief said.

"No," the President replied. "I need to speak with someone else first, and I have to do it myself. Sorry, but this has to be very confidential."

"I understand, sir," Kendall assured him. "So you think these people are really serious?"

"Oh, yes. They're deadly serious."

MACK BOLAN AND RON WAYTON rode the elevators to Malachi Jones's penthouse suite in the Grand Oak complex.

Wayton was miserable. His right arm rested in an improvised sling, and although his broken wrist hurt, he was more concerned about facing Mr. Malachi.

"I'm telling you, man," Wayton said through clenched teeth, "these suckers are going to be pissed off. They didn't act too happy to know I was here. If they saw you get in the elevator—"

"Don't worry," Bolan cut him off. "I've got a way with people. Look how I charmed you."

Wayton rasped a four-letter word under his breath. They had passed through a simple camera surveillance system and Wayton had buzzed the penthouse, getting permission to go up to Malachi Jones's luxury suite. If Mr. Malachi's security people had seen the big white guy enter the elevator, there was sure to be a welcoming committee waiting for them.

The elevator reached its destination, and the doors slid open. Two large African-Americans stood on the threshold, resembling a pair of linebackers in dark suits. Bolan slid both hands into the cargo pockets of his jacket as he nodded at the pair. They glared back in response.

"What the hell is this honkie doing here?" one of them demanded. "You were never very smart, Ron, but you're turning too stupid to live at this rate."

"You don't understand—" Wayton began.

"Will you gentlemen ask Mr. Malachi if he'd be willing to speak with me about making a few hundred thousand dollars in the next few months?" Bolan broke in. "I apologize for not making an appointment, but he's not an easy man to contact. It was hard enough convincing Ron to even bring me here."

One of the thugs looked at Wayton's injured arm as the other shook his head and pointed toward the Executioner.

"Just go back down to the lobby and get out of here," he ordered. "I don't know if you're a cop or what the hell you think you're doing here, but Mr. Malachi is an honest businessman and a respected member of the community. He doesn't need any trouble, and we're not going to let you cause any."

"That's a shame," Bolan replied. "After all this effort to meet him, too."

Suddenly the Executioner shoved Wayton, the push propelling the scrawny dealer from the elevator into one of the strong-arm guys. Both men gasped with surprise, and Wayton howled with pain as his injured arm slammed into the one man's brawny chest.

At the same instant, Bolan stepped from the elevator. The second guard confronted him, growling an obscenity as he reached inside his jacket. The soldier's left hand emerged from his pocket, and he moved closer to the thug, his fist held high. The goon's eyes widened when he saw the Executioner held a hand grenade. With his attention focused on the bomb, the hardman failed to notice Bolan's right arm shot out, driving a short, hard blow with the Y of his hand, between the thumb and forefinger. He hit his opponent in the throat.

The thug choked and staggered backward, both hands raised to his windpipe. Bolan heard the elevator doors hum shut and saw the first guard shove Wayton aside as he unleathered a 9 mm Browning pistol. The Executioner yanked the pin from the grenade.

"Shoot me and I'll drop it," he warned. "This is an M-26 fragmentation grenade. That means you'll have only a couple of seconds before it explodes."

"You're bluffing," the gunman said, sounding uncertain.

"Just try me," Bolan challenged. "Sorry to include you in this, Ron, but I can't leave here until I talk to Jones. If the people I work for find out I failed to even talk to your boss, I'll face a slow, painful death that will make getting splattered by a grenade look like an act of kindness."

"What the hell kind of people do you work for?" the guard asked.

"Believe me, you don't want to know."

"All right," the man conceded as he lowered his weapon. "Wait here. I'll try to get Mr. Malachi."

He headed for a door and rang the bell. The other goon had stopped gagging, but he continued to rub his neck, glaring at Bolan as if he would like to stuff the grenade down the Executioner's throat.

Wayton slowly got to his feet. "You really are an asshole, Favor," he complained.

"Nice guys don't get into the dope trade," Bolan replied with a shrug.

Stanley appeared at the door and spoke with the guard. Jones's top man turned to the Executioner and said, "I don't know any cop who would pull a stunt this crazy. If you want to talk to Mr. Malachi, you have to put that pin back in the grenade. I won't let you in if you don't."

"I'll do it when I'm sure there won't be any more problems with seeing your boss."

Stanley addressed the trio. "You two stay back and don't come in unless you're told to, or you hear trouble," he ordered. "Ron, you're coming in. However this turns out, you've got some explaining to do."

Wayton reluctantly approached. Bolan advanced, holding the pin near the spoon to the grenade as Stanley ushered them into Jones's luxury apartment.

Malachi Jones stood in the center of his living room, arms folded across his chest. He frowned as he looked at the grenade in Bolan's fist, yet he handled the situation more calmly than one would expect.

"Didn't your mother ever tell you it's bad manners to threaten to blow up a host's property?" he inquired.

"Not that I recall," Bolan said, "but we didn't

discuss military hardware much when I was a kid. Things change, Mr. Malachi.''

He stuck the pin back in the grenade. Stanley stood by, his attention divided between the Executioner and his boss, probably watching for a signal if Jones wanted him to take out the visitor. Wayton kept his distance, appearing totally vulnerable and surrounded by hostile forces.

"So who are you and what do you want?" Jones asked.

"As I told Wayton here, you can call me Favor," Bolan said. "That fits our business, because I'm going to do a favor for you and you'll do one for me."

"You seem very sure about that."

"That's because I am. It will be profitable for us both. I represent some people who are interested in buying a large amount of cocaine. You have access to such a supply, and you need buyers. Basic economics."

"I know about supply and demand," Jones said, "but not about selling drugs. I own a number of furniture and carpet stores. I'm an honest businessman."

"You've got a good cover, and it helps to explain why you live well, but we both know you deal in more than household goods. Let's not waste time with this, Mr. Malachi. You're smart and you're careful. The fact that you've never been convicted of a felony proves that. I'm not a cop, and you know it."

"Who gave you this information about me?" Jones asked. "Was it Wayton?"

"No, Ron didn't tell me," Bolan replied. "I learned about you from other sources. The police can't prove you're involved in criminal activities, but they're aware of it. The DEA has a file on you, too. Let's just say I have friends with connections. Arnold Collay is one of your lawyers. He was called in when Ron here got arrested. It's not too hard to figure out what happened. When a bottom-of-the-barrel crack dealer tries to sell high-grade coke to a guy in a limo, it means his boss must have acquired a big supply of the white powder and he wants to move it.''

"But Wayton brought you here.''

"Not willingly,'' the Executioner said. "He pulled a knife and came at me. A bad move. Still, you should know he didn't agree to bring me here until he had a broken wrist and a gun held to his head. On a loyalty level from one to ten, that's got to rank at least a seven.''

The drug dealer shrugged. "How much cocaine are these people you represent interested in buying?''

"About one hundred kilos. Maybe more, if they're happy with your merchandise and they don't have any problems with distribution.''

"That's a lot of coke. I'd say that would be worth about three hundred and fifty thousand dollars.''

"They were thinking of a price tag more like thirty-three, but that can be decided later. For now, they'd like to buy ten kilos and see if everybody is happy with the deal.''

"Three hundred and fifty grand would certainly appeal to me,'' Jones stated. "But they could buy it much cheaper if they went to other sources. A more direct one to South or Central America, for example.''

"They had one of those. The DEA, political turmoil and a gang war between cocaine syndicates all conspired to close down that pipeline, at least for now.''

''How do they expect to make a profit if they spend so much for the product?'' the dealer asked. ''They'd have to have clients willing to pay even more.''

''That's right,'' Bolan confirmed. ''They have a foreign market. Coke is in big demand, and it's difficult to get it there. That means people will pay a lot to get it.''

''Too bad I can't tap into that market directly.''

''Maybe they'll be interested in a partnership in the future. For now, let's see how this deal works out.''

''I have to think about it.''

''I suggest you don't think too long. There are other sources out there. You're not going to find a deal much better than this, Mr. Malachi.''

''It just seems a little too good to be true,'' the dealer said. ''Will you be in Detroit long, Favor?''

''Three days,'' the Executioner replied. ''You do any business with heroin trafficking, by any chance? They're working on a market in that area, as well.''

''Heroin?'' Jones frowned. ''I haven't been involved with that for years.''

''I didn't think so, but it doesn't hurt to ask. Should I contact you tomorrow?''

''Stanley will give you a private phone number, but please be discreet. You never know who might be listening.''

''One can never be too careful,'' Bolan agreed, nodding.

''The method you used to get in here wasn't so

careful,'' Jones said. ''That bluff with the dummy grenade was a bit much.''

''It's a real grenade and I wasn't bluffing. You have a nice day, Mr. Malachi.''

10

"Sometimes I think you're really crazy and the rest of the time I'm sure of it," Hal Brognola declared. "Marching into a drug dealer's lair like that."

The big Fed shook his head as he sat once more at the conference table of the Stony Man War Room. Mack Bolan observed him on the screen of the laptop computer in his room at the White Pine Palace. It was a fancy name for a pretty standard motel, but it was located within easy driving distance of Malachi Jones's building.

"You have to take some risks to get any results," the Executioner stated. "Anyway, I spoke with Jones and he seemed interested. But he's no fool. He's not going to be eager to tell me where he got that cocaine from, not if he knows someone is listening."

"Leo hit town with Gadgets Schwarz," Brognola said. "They have legal authorization to set up surveillance and wiretaps. By the way, our boys in the armor-plated costumes call themselves the Juggernauts. You won't believe who told me that. The President himself."

Bolan was surprised. "They contacted him directly?"

"On a secure line on Air Force One," the big Fed

confirmed. "They sure made an impression on the President, but not one they'd hoped for. He wants us to go after them with everything we've got. We don't have to worry about White House support now."

"Did they tell him what they wanted?"

"Basically they want to take over law enforcement throughout the U.S. They claim they can deal with crime better than anyone else, so they should be in charge. The President said the guy he talked to carried on the conversation in a reasonable manner, although he was making unreasonable demands. He didn't sound like some foaming-at-the-mouth mad dog."

"That's the worse kind. Did this Juggernaut say how killing police and federal agents proves they're such great crime fighters?"

"He implied that the President should just agree those people were killed by the drug dealers and bank robbers in the shoot-outs and to forget about it. He also said they destroyed the cocaine and heroin. Needless to say, the President didn't buy any of that, and he sure didn't appreciate somebody trying to blackmail his way into taking charge of this nation's law enforcement.

"Anyway, we've got a little more to work with now. We know these Juggernauts have to have some pretty good computer and telecommunications expertise. They must be getting information about criminals through police and federal data banks. Contacting the President on Air Force One is a neat trick, too. If they're telling the truth about wanting to be a kind of national police force, that means there are probably some former cops among them. Maybe ex-Feds who got frustrated with the system."

"I imagine you're going to find a hell of a lot of disgruntled cops and ex-cops out there, Hal," Bolan remarked dryly.

"Yeah, but hopefully not too many who'd go to this sort of extreme. Aaron figures we might get lucky looking into cases of cops and Feds who lost their jobs due to brutality or other unacceptable behavior. We might even find somebody who tried to put together some sort of death squad in the past."

"The Juggernauts seem to have been well-trained. Running around in full body armor can't be easy. They must have gotten some sort of conditioning and practice for these raids. That suggests someone with a military background could be involved. Especially someone who had been part of an elite unit like Special Forces or Navy SEALs."

"That's something else to add to our list of possibilities. The biggest advocates of the 'kill 'em all in the name of law and order' tend to be politically to the far right, so we're checking into some of the more extreme groups."

"Anything on the body armor and who may have developed it?"

"We've got a couple of possibilities on that," the big Fed replied. "There were a number of inventors working on protective gear, armor and advanced weaponry who tried to sell their ideas to the military or police organizations. Some of those got vetoed, either because the cold war officially came to an end, or the proposed equipment would simply be too expensive to make or considered too complicated for use in the field. Still others failed when tested and were scrapped before the inventors could try to correct what was wrong with their projects.''

''Any of them working on something similar to the body armor worn by the Juggernauts?'' Bolan asked.

''Actually there were several people who conceived of using spiderweb threads in a manner similar to Kevlar, or woven metal strands. We know the whereabouts and recent activities of most of these inventors. For the most part, they've moved on to other projects or given up the inventing business to concentrate on other ways of making a living. However, we're particularly interested in three scientists involved in weapons and body armor. One moved to Europe and tried to get work with the Belgian military, but they rejected his concepts, as well. He then tried to peddle his inventions in France, and they turned him down, too. Supposedly he's still living in Paris, but he spends a lot of time going to other countries to try to make a deal.''

''And the other two scientists?''

''Nobody is quite sure what happened to either of them,'' Brognola said, leafing through some papers. ''One guy, Andrew Gallow, was working on both body armor and reinforced weapon designs for handling special high-velocity ammunition with hefty grain and armor-piercing capacity. He had proposed a type of spiderweb weave with titanium threads for a bulletproof vest, but his prototype failed to pass tests carried out by the U.S. Army. He claimed the spiderweb strands had to be packed closer together and he wanted to try some different metal alloy combinations, but the military had lost faith in him at that point. He had better luck selling a riot shield to a national police supply distributor. It was made of a clear plastic with a special synthetic resin that hardened the shields to a degree that, and I quote, 'provided impressive protection for an officer and effectively resisted impact from various caliber weapons and 12-gauge buckshot.'"

"So, an expert in the development of devices using advanced plastics as well as metal and experimental spiderweb innovations," Bolan mused. "Gallow sounds like a brilliant man. What happened to him?"

"A good question. The cop shields were successful, but they didn't really catch on due to the high cost of production. Most police departments have similar riot shields, but most aren't really bullet resistant. Still, the majority of police figured what they had would do well enough until Gallow or somebody else provided a superior product at a lower price. Gallow spent the money he made with the shields and just about all the rest of his cash on attempts to improve his old inventions. He was turned down when he tried for government grants to finance his projects. Then he just dropped out of sight. Aaron, his computer system and I all figure Gallow is a good suspect. Too bad none of us has any idea what happened to the man."

"There's another guy on your list?"

"Raul Lopez," the big Fed answered, "another inventor interested in body armor using an exotic weave similar to Gallow's. He tried to convince the government to invest in a Kevlar-style vest with an extra layer of spiderweb for added protection. Apparently this was pretty much theory. He didn't have an actual prototype, and he didn't get too far with it. Lopez had done some previous work on tank construction, armored cars and more conventional flak vests and such. However, he hadn't been getting much work in this country after the hoopla over the Gulf War wore off. Then he vanished, but they think he may have used a fake passport and disguise to head for South America. According to his file, he speaks Spanish fluently and is semifluent in Portuguese and French.''

"So he may have gone south to look for contracts with major arms manufacturers in Brazil or Argentina,'' Bolan guessed. "Both countries sell a lot of weaponry to international markets.''

"That seems to be the most popular theory about the guy. Lopez is still a member of the U.S. Army reserves and holds a top-secret crypto clearance. That's why he may have used a fake passport and disguise. Seems he was always sort of paranoid, accusing the Army and the CIA of spying on him and trying to prevent him from leaving the U.S.''

"What source did you get this information from?''

"From psychological evaluations by Army intelligence and the CIA. They should know if Lopez was paranoid, after spying on him for so long. Anyway, it's possible he might still be here in the States, working for the Juggernauts. Gallow might be a more likely choice for us, but as we don't know what happened to either of them, it's impossible to know. Hell, the inventors of the Juggernauts' fancy gear might be somebody we haven't even got on the list.''

"Seems like we're coming up with more questions than answers,'' Bolan said. "That's becoming typical of this mission.''

"I don't recall having had a mission quite like this

before," Brognola commented. "You've usually been up against opponents who fall down and die when you shoot them."

"Cowboy gave me these armor-piercing bullets. Hopefully that'll make the next encounter with the Juggernauts different from the previous ones."

"I sure hope so. You watch your back, Striker. Even if you don't come across those bastards in high-tech tin cans, you still have to deal with Malachi Jones and his crew. He might not be a big-time criminal, but he's smart and certainly dangerous, as well."

"I don't plan on getting killed in Detroit," Bolan assured him. "I'll be in touch, Hal."

They signed off. Bolan decided he could use a hot shower and a change of clothes. He first slipped out of the shoulder holster rig that held the Beretta, then slid his belt off. He checked the inside of the belt for a small slit that concealed a handcuff key, worn at the small of his back when the belt was in place, making sure the key was still intact.

Bolan set the belt on the bed, next to the ammunition pouches and the Beretta. He wondered how effective his weapon would be against the Juggernauts' armor. He recalled the gun battle in Pittsburgh, where his trusted pistol had seemed like a pellet gun against a group of gun-toting rhinos. Even with Kissinger's special 9 mm Parabellums, he couldn't be certain he would do any better if he clashed with the Juggernauts again, or if he would even survive another encounter.

"I never figured I'd die of old age, anyway," he muttered.

MALACHI JONES WATCHED the small TV set in the back of his limo. The stock market hadn't improved since he'd read the morning paper. Frustrated, he switched off the set and gazed out the window.

He smiled at the sight of his favorite restaurant. The management and staff at Lake Bistro always treated him well. Of course, he was a good customer who tipped well, but he knew they genuinely liked him, admiring the fact that he was a local business-man who had made it from the ghetto to a penthouse. The folks at Lake Bistro thought he had done that by selling furniture and carpets. Sometimes Jones wished that was true, that his fortune hadn't been made deal-ing in drugs and stolen merchandise. Sometimes he thought about making enough money to set himself up without having to deal in any illegal business. He would try to make up for some of the sins he had committed, perhaps starting a drug rehab center or a child-care clinic to help working mothers. Yet, he re-alized those were things he considered only during rare moments of guilt. He liked the power he held as much as his wealth. He would never make enough money to be satisfied. He had made his choices long ago and knew he would have to live with them.

Stanley steered the limo into the parking lot. They made their way into the restaurant, where the hostess recognized Jones.

"We have your table reserved, sir," she said. "A Mr. Webster called earlier to say he couldn't make it. He left a phone number for you to call him."

"Thank you," Jones said, taking the number from the hostess and heading for the pay phone. His call was answered on the second ring.

"Sorry I couldn't make it," Raymond Stylles said, "but you seem to be attracting too much attention these days."

"You may be right," Jones admitted. "Do we arrange a meeting for another time?"

"I'm a busy man, so I'll tell you what I've got now. Your business has already gotten a big boost from the cocaine shipment I brought you. How would you like fifteen kilos of uncut heroin, as well? I'm practically giving it away at fifty thousand. Don't haggle because I won't go any lower."

"Heroin?"

"Don't tell me that's beneath you, Jones. Drugs are drugs and money is money."

"Yes, I know. It's just that a man came to me today who wants to buy a large amount of coke, and he's willing to pay top dollar for it. He also asked if I did any business in heroin."

"Do you know him?" Stylles demanded. "How'd he find out about you?"

"He calls himself Favor. He didn't act like a cop—"

"I didn't ask you that. I don't like it. A coincidence like this makes me very suspicious. Can you find this Favor character?"

"Probably. I can find almost anyone in the city if I have to, but I'm supposed to hear from him tomorrow."

"Forget that. I want him taken care of tonight. Too much is at stake, and we can't afford any mistakes."

"If he's a cop or a Fed, this may not be the best way to handle it. I mean, that's going to bring some heat down on me, Webster. Maybe I could stall him until we find out who he is.''

''Just find him and take care of him. You'll hear from me later.''

Stylles hung up. Jones sighed and returned the phone to its cradle. Suddenly he didn't seem to have much of an appetite.

11

Zachary St. John's paratrooper boots pounded on the tiled floor of the corridor. He marched past rows of doors until he reached Andrew Gallow's special section. He opened the door to the scientist's office without bothering to knock. The room was empty.

St. John moved to the research lab where Gallow spent most of his time on various projects. He found the man seated on a stool, his eyes glued to a microscope.

Gallow heard the footsteps and raised his head. He groped for his glasses, barely able to recognize St. John until he'd put them on. "You shouldn't come in here unannounced," he said. "I could have been using explosives, electricity or some dangerous chemicals."

"Stylles called to say he's made a change of plans," St. John stated. "He's not going for the target in Milwaukee. Instead he's contacted the troops in his unit to meet him in Detroit."

"Did he give a reason?"

"It's something to do with that drug dealer. Apparently he's made a serious mistake that could put our whole operation in jeopardy. I knew we shouldn't have let Stylles talk us into doing business with that man. I don't like dealing with drugs, period, nor do I like Stylles changing strategy in the middle of a mission.''

"There must be a reason for it, Captain.''

"The reason is Stylles thinks he runs this show, and we're supposed to take orders from him. I started this place before Stylles ever heard of it, Andy. You told me we needed Stylles, said he knew how to get information and had connections that could help us go after the vermin in society.''

"You have to admit he has done that. We couldn't have located those gangster strongholds on our own. Besides, if we intend to have a national police force, we need someone who served with a federal law-enforcement agency,'' Gallows said, defending himself.

St. John grunted and began to pace the floor, his hands clasped behind his back. As usual, he wore his fatigue uniform. He never tired of being a soldier. When he hadn't fit into the U.S. Army, he'd tried to create one of his own. Now, he felt he was losing control of his command to Raymond Stylles.

"I don't think he should have spoken to the President, either,'' he said. "It's too early for that. The President and others in the federal government aren't prepared to surrender control of national law enforcement to us this soon. We have to prove we can accomplish what no one else can. We have to get the American public firmly behind us before we can expect the government to agree to our demands. That damn sure won't happen if we keep killing police officers and federal agents.''

"That was unfortunate,'' Gallow agreed, "but you

and your team were forced to kill those law officers in Pittsburgh. It couldn't be avoided. You said so yourself.''

''It could have been if Stylles hadn't insisted we hit those idiot Anarchist bank robbers as our first target. They got a lot of publicity when they claimed some sort of political motivation, which was a lie, and seemed to be a sort of throwback to the days of John Dillinger, or Bonnie and Clyde. Stylles told us the high degree of interest in the gang would gain us points when we took them out. He should have known the police would also piece together information and learn the Anarchists were using that old plant for a hideout.''

''You could have called off the raid when you saw the police outside the plant, but you decided to go ahead with the plan.''

''I completed my mission,'' St. John insisted. ''I didn't take it upon myself to change what we had planned. Stylles is making too many decisions on his own, and that puts all of us in danger.''

''We'll have to talk to Ray about this when he gets back,'' Gallow said. ''I'm not sure there really is a problem, but we do need to discuss this and prevent our leadership from becoming divided and thus weakened.''

''We need to take a more realistic look at what we're doing, too,'' St. John added. ''The body armor you invented is fantastic, but it doesn't make us invincible, immortal, or anything more than men. We keep pushing our luck, what with the combined efforts of the federal government and various police departments hunting us. Stylles seems to forget that.''

Gallow frowned. He *knew* his armor made them more than human. Obviously St. John failed to realize that. But there was nothing to be gained by arguing with the captain. After all, why should the creator of gods debate with someone who still considered himself a mere mortal?

MACK BOLAN PULLED his Honda rental into the parking space in front of his motel-room door. Earlier, he had met briefly with Leo Turrin and Gadgets Schwarz. They had begun surveillance on Malachi Jones, but so far it hadn't accomplished much. It hadn't been necessary to place a wiretap on the drug dealer's phone line, because the Detroit PD narcotics division had already done so. Turrin was going to meet with the head narc to try to gain cooperation with the help of his Justice ID.

Schwarz had planted a microphone transmitter under Jones's limo and even tailed him to a restaurant. That, too, had yielded nothing, which wasn't surprising. Surveillance generally took time to produce results. Schwarz had also said reception on the radio telemetry equipment had been poor. Even standard forms of communication had been disturbed by unusually high levels of static, which suggested some sort of atmospheric interference.

The Executioner killed the headlights and switched off the engine. After locking the car, he walked toward his room, digging in his pocket for the room key. He stopped in midstride: the venetian blinds at his window were closed. He had left them open.

He went for the Beretta holstered under his arm. From the corner of his eye, he saw a shadow move in the parking lot. Bolan spun, spotted a large black man standing between two vehicles, his pistol leveled. The Executioner recognized the guy and the weapon. They had met in the hall to Malachi Jones's penthouse.

"Get your hands up, Favor," the gunman ordered.

"What the hell is this about?" Bolan asked.

The motel door opened. The other strong-arm guard from Jones's penthouse stood on the threshold, Ron Wayton beside him. He held a .38 snub-nose revolver in his left fist, his broken right wrist encased in a plaster cast.

"You just happen to be in the neighborhood?" Bolan said to Wayton.

"Get in here!" the young dealer growled, motioning with his weapon.

Bolan entered, followed by the man with the Browning. The second guard glared at the Executioner as he rubbed his throat, clearly wishing to pay him back for the "Y" of the hand stroke he had received earlier.

The gunman closed the door. His companion raised a fist and prepared to throw a punch.

"I'm going to bust up this honkie!"

"Not yet," his partner insisted. "Frisk him first. Get his guns, hand grenades and whatever else he's carrying. He's a slick sucker, so do a good job, Oscar."

"You're going to tell us who you really are, Favor," Wayton said as he pointed the short barrel of his revolver at Bolan's face, "and what you are. The stuff we found in the closet looks like it belongs to some kind of federal pig."

"What stuff?" the pistolman asked.

"Oh, some kind of fancy binoculars," Wayton said, "a big knife in a sheath stuck in an Army boot, a couple of boxes of 9 mm rounds and something that looked like a portable computer."

"A laptop," the guy in charge of the trio remarked. "A lot of people have them these days."

"Not like this one, Jim. Take a look."

The man stuck the Browning in his belt as he approached the bed where Bolan's special gear, including the computer, lay sprawled across the spread. Oscar shoved Bolan against a wall as Wayton stepped closer, his .38 pointed at the Executioner's head.

"Hands on the wall and spread 'em," Oscar rasped.

Bolan obeyed. Oscar's hands roughly patted him down, soon locating the 93-R under his left arm. The guy snorted and slid his hand inside Bolan's jacket, his attention focused on the task.

That was the best distraction the Executioner could hope for under the circumstances. He suddenly pushed away from the wall, slamming his elbow into Oscar's face. The blow connected with the hood's upper lip and drove him back into Wayton. A muffled gunshot sounded, and Bolan turned to see Oscar's body stiffen and his head jerk back, eyes wide with surprise. Blood spurted from a bullet hole beneath his chin. Wayton stood frozen behind the man, smoke rising from the revolver in his hand. Wayton had triggered his weapon when Bolan took action, accidentally shooting Oscar through the back of the neck.

Bolan jumped the shocked Wayton, grabbing the dealer's weapon with his right hand. With his left, he delivered a short, hard punch to Wayton's chin. Suddenly he saw Jim draw his Browning.

Without loosening his hold on Wayton's gun hand, the Executioner pressed down on the petty crook's index finger, firing the .38. Jim shuddered, then stared at the crimson patch on his shirtfront. His knees buckled and he slumped to the floor, his weapon slipping from his lifeless fingers.

Bolan relieved Wayton of his revolver and swung a backfist to the man's face. The dealer staggered from the blow, a ribbon of blood trickling from his nostril.

Desperately he turned and yanked open the motel-room door.

Bolan moved rapidly. Grabbing Wayton's left hand, he shoved it into the space between the door and frame, then thrust his weight against the door.

The petty criminal screamed as the door slammed on his wrist and hand, crunching bone. Bolan pulled back, and Wayton fell to the floor, whimpering as he stared at his broken left wrist and mashed fingers, trying to cradle it with his cast-covered right hand.

The Executioner headed for the closet, got out his suitcase and began stowing his gear. He closed the case, picked up the laptop and headed for the door. From the floor, Wayton looked up at him, his face filled with fear.

"You really are having a bad day," Bolan said, "aren't you, Ron?"

He left the room and hurried to his rental.

12

Good brandy had to be one of the finest things in life, Malachi Jones thought as he raised the balloon glass to his nose and inhaled slowly. He took his first sip and closed his eyes to better appreciate the taste. The strident ring of the telephone cut into the moment.

"Damn. Couldn't those idiots wait until morning to call?"

Stanley hurried to the phone and grabbed the handset, aware his boss didn't appreciate being disturbed when relaxing in his den. Jones remained seated in the armchair, clad in a comfortable silk robe and slippers. He guessed the call was from the trio sent to dispatch the man who called himself Favor. The job had been assigned to Jim and Oscar because they would recognize Favor. Ron Wayton was permitted to go along as a way to redeem himself for his recent mistakes.

Jones didn't like to use violence, but he accepted that it was a necessary part of his business. He was reluctant to have anyone killed and was particularly opposed to the termination of someone who might be a cop or a Fed. It was bad for business; the law-and-order boys got very upset when one of their own was taken down. They would want revenge, which meant they'd triple their efforts against his operation to achieve it.

"It's your lawyer, Arnold Collay," Stanley announced. "He says it's important, Mr. Malachi."

His attorney wouldn't be calling him at that hour if it wasn't important, Jones realized. He set his brandy aside and took the phone. The voice of the Harvard-educated criminal defense attorney came over the line.

"Your friend Ronald Wayton called my office, and my answering service relayed his message to me," he began. "He's been arrested again. He hasn't even been out on bail for a full twenty-four hours and already he's in trouble. I'm not so sure I want to continue to represent this man, Malachi. A plea of entrapment on a drug sale is one thing. Double homicide is another."

"Double homicide?" Jones asked, surprised.

"Wayton was picked up by the police at the White Pine Palace when they arrived to investigate reports of gunshots at the motel. They found Wayton and two bodies. Both had apparently been killed by a medium-caliber firearm, most probably the .38 revolver found at the scene. Wayton also had half a dozen cartridges of this caliber in his pocket. That sort of thing sure doesn't help his case."

"Do you know who the victims were?"

"According to their drivers' licenses, their names were James Holmes and Oscar Sparks. Both men were armed. Neither carried gun permits."

"Sons of—" Jones hissed.

Collay cut him off. "You may recognize their names, but I'm not sure I want to know about that.

Wayton said he shot one of them by accident, and another man grabbed his hand and made him shoot the second victim. He's going to need a better story than that before he goes to court. About all that is in his favor is the fact that his wrist is broken, which suggests there could have been another person present at the time of the shooting. I understand his other wrist had been broken just a few hours before.''

"You mean he has two broken wrists?"

"Yes. At any rate, Wayton has got himself in a pretty bad mess here. I don't like to refer to any case as hopeless, but he's going to serve some time even if he doesn't get convicted for murder. I don't particularly care to have a case like this on my sheet. I doubt he's important enough to you to pay the sort of salary I'd want to handle this myself."

"No, he isn't, but I need to think about this, Arnold. This comes as quite a shock, you understand. Should I call you tomorrow, around ten?"

"I'll be in court most of the day. We have a break at noon. I can call you then."

"Fine," Jones confirmed. "Thanks for letting me know about this."

He hung up, cursing under his breath. What the hell had happened at that motel? Everything had gone wrong. Jim and Oscar were dead, and Wayton had been arrested, while that man Favor was apparently still alive and well. Webster wouldn't be happy.

The sudden roar of automatic gunfire galvanized Jones. He jumped from his seat and stared at the front door to the penthouse. The shooting came from the outside hallway, but he hadn't been alerted to anyone coming up in the elevator. Wondering how they got in was a moot point, he decided, rushing toward a bookcase. He yanked open a drawer and scooped up a Walther PPK pistol. He jacked the slide to chamber a round, aware he hadn't used a gun in years. With relief, he saw Stanley draw his own revolver and point it at the door.

Jones hesitated, not sure what to do. He had never seriously considered the possibility that anyone would attack his home. Any threat was supposed to be handled by the complex's security or his own bodyguards. But his men stationed in the hall weren't armed with submachine guns, so whoever had launched this attack would probably barrel right through them.

Then the door burst open, and a figure marched across the threshold. Stanley aimed his gun, but froze when he saw the intruder. The armored gunman stepped closer, turning his helmeted head toward the bodyguard as he brought his weapon to bear. Stanley still seemed unable to believe what was happening. The Juggernaut blasted a short volley, the 10 mm slugs tearing into the man and hurling his body across the room to slam into a wall. Stanley slid to the floor, an expression of amazement on his face.

"My God," Jones gasped as he stared at Stanley's corpse.

The armor-clad killer turned to face him. Two more figures clad in protective gray and helmets appeared behind him. Jones gripped the Walther in both hands and desperately squeezed the trigger, firing into the chest of Stanley's killer. Sparks revealed the bullets were on target, yet his opponent didn't even flinch.

"Who the hell are you?" the dealer cried out.

Laughter met his question, the sound muffled by the Juggernaut's helmet. The other gray assassins advanced, submachine guns pointed at Jones. Their leader raised a gloved hand, telling his men to halt. Jones began to back away, moving until he banged his elbow on the corner of a stereo unit set on a shelf of an entertainment center. He glanced at the pistol in his fist, and, realizing it was useless against the attackers' body armor, tossed it aside.

"Okay," he said, "let's talk about a deal."

He turned his body slightly as he spoke, using it to conceal his hand movement as he quickly pressed the record button on the stereo. He had raised his hands until they were above his head.

"What do you people want?"

The Juggernaut leader stepped closer as he began to speak. "We have to shut you down and wipe you out," came the muffled, yet strangely familiar voice. "I wish we could have spared you longer, Malachi. We would have had to do this eventually, of course, but I had planned to leave you be as long as possible."

"Webster!" the drug dealer exclaimed with sudden recognition. "What the hell is this about? Why are you doing this?"

"It's a long story and we really don't have time to go into it," Raymond Stylles said. "I'm sorry this has to be done. I almost liked you, Malachi, even if you are a drug-selling sack of dirt."

"*You* sold drugs to *me*, you damn hypocrite!" Jones yelled. "If you're going to kill me, just do it, but don't pretend you're any better than I am."

"My motives are different. But I have to agree with you that I should just kill you and get it over with."

"No, Webster—"

"It might be better if you turned around," Stylles suggested. "You really don't want to see it coming, do you?"

Jones realized he would accomplish nothing by trying to reason with the killers. To beg would simply make his final moments on earth pointlessly humiliating. He turned to face the wall and closed his eyes.

MACK BOLAN STEERED the Honda with one hand as he keyed the handset to a radio transceiver on the seat beside him. He was trying to contact Leo Turrin and Gadgets Schwarz, but all he could get was static. He switched on the car radio and discovered more interference. He changed channels but got the same result. The police frequency was also jammed.

Something was blocking radio transmissions on every level. The Executioner guessed it was probably an atmospheric condition of some kind, but there was nothing he could do about it, and he couldn't afford to waste time driving all over Detroit trying to find Turrin and Schwarz. He had business to take care of, and he intended to do it with or without backup.

Bolan had left the White Pine Palace motel after his encounter with Malachi Jones's hardmen and used the police scanner before the static had set in. He'd learned that the cops had arrived at the motel and arrested Ron Wayton. He had heard no mention of any eyewitness descriptions of himself or his vehicle. He gave thanks for the apathetic "don't get involved'' attitude of the big city. At least he didn't have to worry about the police looking for him.

The Executioner had a particular quarry in mind: Malachi Jones had to have sent those three thugs to kill him, and he wanted to know why.

He approached Jones's building, circling the block to be sure the police weren't present and to do a preliminary recon of the area. Ideally he would have liked more time before he made his move on the location, but he didn't want to give the dealer any opportunity to make a break for it.

Little traffic moved along the street as he finished his revolution. The night sky seemed to have become brighter. He glanced up, noticing an ivory-colored shaft of light bisecting the firmament that seemed to be part of a large cloud formation. Perhaps that was the weather condition that was causing the dense static in radio transmissions.

As Bolan zeroed in on the complex, his vehicle's headlights picked out a box-shaped van parked by the curb. An alarm sounded inside his head. The body of the van appeared thicker than normal, with patches of scarred metal covered by a thin layer of gray paint. He recalled the reinforced van used by the Juggernauts in Pittsburgh and similar rigs reported at their raids in L.A. and Chicago.

He pulled into an alley across the street from the building and switched off the engine, emerging from the Honda and facing the complex. Three figures stepped from the entrance to the building. His face turned grim as he took in the gray body armor and helmets worn by the trio, the subguns, side arms and ammunition pouches they carried.

He hadn't expected to encounter the Juggernaut killers, but he responded without hesitation. Drawing his Beretta, he held it in a firm Weaver combat grip as he tracked their progress toward the van.

He took aim and squeezed the trigger. The Beretta unleashed a 3-round burst, recoiling in his hands with twice the kick he was accustomed to, due to the hot load ammunition. Then he saw that he had hit his intended target. A Juggernaut had taken the three 9 mm slugs in the side of the helmet. He staggered sideways into a clipped hedge and tumbled out of Bolan's view.

"One down," the Executioner said as the remaining Juggernauts turned toward him. Acquiring a new target, he triggered another 3-round salvo. The Parabellum rounds slammed into the gray breastplate of the second enemy. The man stumbled backward as if he'd been punched in the chest. He whirled his arms, trying to maintain his balance. The sight would have been almost comical, but Bolan didn't crack a smile. The Juggernaut didn't go down.

The third gunman raised his weapon as Bolan sprinted from the alley. The subgun bellowed, unleashing several rounds in the vicinity of where the soldier had been just a moment before. He heard the metallic twang as projectiles pierced the body of the Honda. Bolan kept moving, seeking cover by a Ford Escort parked at the curb. He crouched and fired another burst at the enemy, but he failed to find target acquisition.

An explosion roared from the alley as one of the Juggernaut's projectiles found the Honda's gas tank. Shards of metal and broken glass were hurled into the street, and flames shot from the mouth of the alley. At the same instant, a volley of enemy bullets shattered the display window of a shoe store behind Bolan, the entire glass pane dissolving with a crash.

The term ''armor piercing'' was supposed to apply to Bolan's ammunition as well, but Kissinger's hot loads were no match for the Juggernauts' incredible protective gear. The gunner Bolan thought he'd taken out with a head shot was back on his feet, weapon up and ready. The trio of rounds to his helmet had served only to knock him off balance, not kill or even wound him. Rounds hammered into the Executioner's shelter, slugs puncturing the body of the Escort as if the vehicle were made of tinfoil. The hood sprang open and water spurted from the pierced radiator. Two bullets punched through the vehicle near Bolan's head, scoring on a brick wall behind him.

The soldier raised his head, darting a glance over the frame of the battered Ford. A single Juggernaut had marched into the street, moving toward Bolan's position, aware they had the man pinned down and clearly determined to get a final, telling shot at him.

Bolan fired his Beretta, nailing the enemy with another direct hit to the torso. The Juggernaut swayed from the impact as he returned fire, his shots raking the wall well above the soldier's head as they went wildly off course. Angered, but apparently unharmed, the enforcer kept moving forward.

''Dave!'' a muffled voice yelled from the street. ''Get back here! We have to haul out before the cops come!''

The Juggernaut ignored the order, continuing to walk toward Bolan's cover, firing his subgun as he advanced. The windows to the Escort shattered, and Bolan ducked as glass shards fell across his back. Although his special ammunition seemed useless against the Juggernauts' body armor, the Executioner knew he had no option but to try again. Aiming the Beretta at his opponent's helmeted head, he squeezed the trigger, sending a triburst slamming into the tinted visor.

Cracks spiderwebbed on the thick plastic. The submachine gun slipped from the Juggernaut's gloved hand as he swayed on unsteady legs, two bullet holes visible in the visor. The enforcer raised both hands to the helmet, then suddenly toppled backward, his armored body crashing to the ground. The loosened helmet fell from his head and rolled away.

"He's killed Dave!" a voice roared. "The bastard's killed him!"

Bolan didn't waste time congratulating himself on finally bringing down one of his armor-plated adversaries. He bolted from behind the Escort, taking advantage of the momentary distraction as the remaining enemy realized one of them had been slain, despite their invincible, protective gear.

The Executioner sprinted to the shattered display window of the shoe store and dived through the opening. He hit the floor in a forward roll as a wave of submachine gun fire ripped into the store, sending shoes and cardboard boxes hopping from the shelves. Several showered Bolan's position, but he barely noticed as he adopted a kneeling stance, his weapon aimed at the display window.

The Juggernauts would be less eager to pursue him, Bolan realized. They had just discovered they were still mortal inside their fancy armor, and they also needed to escape before the police arrived. He weighed the situation and guessed they would probably choose to flee and avoid more casualties rather than attempt to hunt him down to avenge their fallen comrade.

Then he recalled that the enforcers had used grenades, as well as firearms, in previous raids. An explosion inside the shoe store would be devastating. He glanced about, but saw no available cover aside from flimsy aluminum and plastic shelves, a plywood counter and some wall racks. The enemy had ceased fire, but he couldn't assume they had left. He headed for the rear of the store, to a door marked Employees Only. He turned the knob, but the door was locked.

A noise at the front of the store drew his attention; the Juggernauts' reinforced van had pulled up, halting beside the ravaged Escort. Whirling, the Executioner slammed a boot to the door, shattering the lock with a hard, well-placed kick. He rushed into a storage area, sprinted past rows of shoe boxes and headed for a back exit. The metal security door was designed to keep out intruders, not to trap anyone inside. Bolan slammed the bar latch and the door swung open.

He hit the outside just as dual explosions—one rolling into the other—reverberated within the store. He felt the violent vibrations against the metal door, and the entire building seemed to tremble from the blast. He guessed the Juggernauts had hurled two grenades through the display window, which was a solid tactic. A person might reach one grenade in time to throw it back at the enemy before it exploded, but the chances of getting two would be almost nonexistent.

Bolan stood in the dark alley, inhaling deeply to try to slow his pulse. The blood rushed in his veins, the result of both the stresses and stimulation of combat. He guessed that the enemy was almost certainly in too great a hurry to hang around to make sure he was dead. Still, his senses were primed for danger as he headed through the alley, his Beretta up and leading. He hugged the shadows until he reached the mouth of the alley, sirens wailing in the distance as he emerged. A few onlookers stood on the sidewalk, staring at the destruction that littered the street.

Bolan holstered his pistol and removed a badge with a Justice Department ID from a jacket pocket. He clipped it to his lapel in case the police wanted to know who Mike Belasko was and what he was doing at the scene. The soldier reached the corner of the street and examined the scene.

His Honda rental still burned, and the smashed remains of the Ford lay scattered in front of the shoe store, its interior trashed into oblivion by the enemy grenades. There was no sign of the Juggernauts or their vehicle.

The body of their slain companion was also gone. Bolan guessed the enemy had taken the body for reasons more practical than sentimental: the Juggernauts wouldn't want the dead man to be identified or the body armor to fall into the hands of the authorities. However, they had missed something in their haste. Bolan picked up the helmet that had rolled into the gutter.

He turned it over in his hands. It was heavy, but not as heavy as he would have guessed in order to be so durable. The tinted visor had been secured with steel bolts, blood and bullet holes now marring the front. The metal surface of the helmet was still smooth, and he could see no scratches or nicks on it.

A blue Dodge screeched to a halt by the curb. Bolan recognized Gadgets Schwarz behind the wheel, and he hurried over to the passenger side and climbed in.

"I tried to get here sooner," Schwarz explained. "I saw part of the gun battle through a surveillance scope, but I was set up more than a mile away and I couldn't get through the damn traffic."

"Let's just get out of here," Bolan urged. "Did you get a heat-sensor reading on the Juggernauts' van on your way over here? We might be able to track them if you did."

"Hell, I didn't expect those bastards to hit Jones. I didn't expect you to show up, either. Why didn't you contact me before you charged over here?"

"I tried, but I couldn't get through. When I went looking for Jones, I didn't know the Juggernauts would be there. Too bad they got away, but at least one of them isn't breathing anymore."

Schwarz glanced over at the helmet Bolan held. Police cars, with their lights flashing, and firetrucks passed them on their way to the battle scene, and Schwarz turned down a side street to avoid them.

"So you took out one of them," he remarked. "Guess their armor isn't so tough after all."

"Tough enough," Bolan assured him. "Cowboy will want to see this helmet. I'm glad you came along when you did. I would have had a hell of a time trying to explain walking around with this thing under my arm."

"What happened to your rental car?"

"They blew it up," the Executioner answered. "I knew I was going to have trouble with a Japanese car in Detroit."

13

Aaron Kurtzman rolled into the Stony Man War Room, where Mack Bolan sat at the conference table with Hal Brognola. He nodded a greeting and waved a printout at the pair.

"I've got a meteorological report here on atmospheric conditions over the state of Michigan in general, and the Detroit area in particular," he announced. "I found out what caused all that static and interference with the radio communications that prevented you from being able to contact Leo or Gadgets last night."

"It affected police and civilian radio broadcasts, as well," Bolan said. "There was no thunderstorm moving in that I could see. In fact the sky was pretty clear, aside from that strange luminous cloud."

Kurtzman nodded. "A mother-of-pearl cloud. It's a fairly rare phenomenon, similar to the northern lights. Basically it caused radio waves to get drowned out by thick static."

"But it didn't affect regular telephone communications?" Bolan asked. "I'm just curious how the police were called to the scene of the gun battle and whether the wiretap on Malachi Jones's telephone line would have picked up anything aside from static last night.''

"Telephone lines along poles or underground cables were not affected," Kurtzman answered. "Sometimes the old-style technology works better than high tech. Actually Jones did get a call from that lawyer guy, Arnold Collay. He was talking about your pal Ron Wayton and the other two characters who tried to take you out at the motel.''

"Poor Ron," Bolan said sardonically. "It wasn't a very good night for the Malachi Jones syndicate.''

"That's a fact," Brognola confirmed. "Jones and three of his bodyguards were found dead at his penthouse. Apparently the Juggernauts deactivated the security system, then took out the guys in the hall, broke down the door to Jones's apartment and killed him and his bodyguard. Then you arrived just as they were coming out of the place. The Juggernauts had apparently supplied cocaine from the L.A. job to Jones, but then they turned on him. They must have decided he was a liability.''

"It was probably after Jones talked to me about a drug deal," Bolan said. "He seemed interested in the offer I made, but then he sent his men to waste me. He must have been told to do that after he spoke with a high-ranking Juggernaut.''

"Leo and Gadgets had Jones under surveillance. So did the Detroit narc division. As far as they know, he wasn't in contact with anyone between your visit and the attempt to take you out.''

"That just proves the Juggernauts are smart," Bolan replied. "If they weren't, we would have nailed them already. They must have guessed Jones was being watched and his phone tapped. Gadgets followed him to a restaurant earlier that evening. We know that he didn't meet with anyone there, but he could have used a pay phone to talk to a Juggernaut commander.''

"You're probably right,'' Brognola said. "How did Jones manage to find you so easily? You didn't tell him you were staying at the White Pine Palace.''

"No, but Detroit was his town. A white guy comes to Detroit, uses a rented car from the airport and checks into a motel near Malachi's place. It wouldn't be that hard to find me. He sent Wayton and the two bodyguards I'd met outside his penthouse so they could make a positive ID when they saw me. I guess he wanted to make sure the wrong guy wasn't killed. However, none of them were really hit men, especially Wayton. They should have taken me out as soon as they had the drop on me.''

"Lucky they didn't,'' Kurtzman remarked.

"I could have arranged a decent safehouse before I arrived in Detroit, but I wanted Jones to think I was exactly what I appeared to be—a go-between for a party interested in selling cocaine to a source abroad. My guess is he mentioned me to the Juggernauts and told them I was looking for heroin as well as coke. That must have seemed too great a coincidence, seeing as they had just acquired some heroin from their hit on the Russians in Chicago. They realized I was a threat and decided it was time to get rid of Jones, as well.''

"Leo used his Justice Department clout to take charge of the investigation into Jones's homicide and everything connected with it,'' Brognola said. "He was with the Detroit police last night, while you were encountering hardmen with and without armor plating.''

"The ones without are easier," Bolan stated dryly. "That body armor even withstood Cowboy's special Parabellum hot loads. Fortunately the plastic visor didn't hold up so well. Is Cowboy still examining the helmet?''

"Yeah," Brognola said, "and he's impressed with it, too. I'm beginning to think you'll need to use a rocket launcher on these bastards.''

"That has crossed my mind," Bolan admitted, "but we can't use rocket or grenade launchers as long as the Juggernauts continue to carry out their missions in populated areas. We couldn't use weapons that would put hundreds of innocent lives at risk.''

"Too bad they don't go by the same rules," Kurtzman commented. "The Juggernauts haven't shown any concern for innocent bystanders when they blast away with their armor-piercing bullets or lob grenades.''

"We're not them," Bolan replied. "If we have to destroy a city block and everyone on it in order to take out one terrorist, then we're no better than they are. I've seen war fought that way. They call it 'acceptable losses.' Killing innocent people can never be acceptable.''

"Let's hope Cowboy can come up with something that will work against the Juggernauts without putting people at more risk than necessary," the big Fed said. "We might be able to minimize such risk, but we can't eliminate it, Mack.''

"I've got to head back to my computers," Kurtzman said. "I've got the artificial-intelligence systems evaluating known information, strong theories and suspected transportation methods used by the Juggernauts to try to determine a likely spot for their home base. Also, we're trying to determine what their next target might be."

"Computerized clairvoyance," Brognola joked.

"Hey," Kurtzman said, defending his operation, "my machines work on available data, mathematical probability and logic. You might recall we've been pretty successful with this method in the past."

"Okay," the big Fed replied. "You get back to that high-tech Nostradamus and let us know if you get lucky. If any information rolls in from Leo in Detroit, be sure to put it through to the Cowboy's terminal."

"You'd think I was running a switchboard," Kurtzman grumbled as he rolled toward the elevator.

THE JUGGERNAUT HELMET lay on a counter in John Kissinger's workshop. The weapons expert sat on a stool near the trophy and peered into a microscope. He looked up as Bolan and Brognola entered his domain.

"This is the damnedest headgear I've ever seen," he said. "If you'd told me it came from another planet, I wouldn't be too quick to dismiss that claim."

"The thing I shot was definitely human," Bolan assured him. "At least as far as you can apply that term when it comes to killers like that."

"So what have you learned from studying this thing?" Brognola asked, pointing at the helmet.

"Okay," Kissinger began, "we know that the Juggernauts' armor is extremely hard and able to stand up to incredible punishment and stress.''

"Like being hit by so-called armor-piercing bullets?'' Bolan inquired with a raised eyebrow.

"The ammunition I gave you *is* armor piercing,'' Kissinger insisted. "Those Parabellum rounds punched right through double layers of Kevlar when I tested it. The body armor is obviously even tougher than we suspected. You appreciate that more than anybody else, Mack.''

"I can't say I appreciate it, but I know it to be true.''

"Well, we knew the metals used in the armor included titanium and rhodium, as well as woven spiderweb strands. What we didn't know until now, having examined the helmet, is that the outer layer of the armor is largely a rhodium alloy, with the second layer a titanium alloy and the third a chemically treated spiderweb mesh. I had to use a diamond cutter just to scrape off samples for the microscope.''

"That's all very interesting,'' Brognola said, "but does it help us find a weakness in the damn armor or not?''

Kissinger slapped his palm against the helmet and said, "Not much weakness to find here. The metal and web combination is pretty formidable. In fact the helmet might be the toughest item of the Juggernauts' gear. Its curved design is more inclined to deflect a projectile than a flat surface. That's why bullets will often bounce right off a curved windshield. There have been plenty of documented cases of bullets actually bouncing off a person's skull if it struck at the right angle.''

"The visor didn't hold up so well," Brognola noted.

"That might be a weak spot compared to the rest," Kissinger admitted. "The visor is made of a high-tech plastic, similar to the type used for the portholes on the space shuttle."

"Still, it's not all that vulnerable," Bolan said. "I had to nail the enforcer at close range with three rounds to penetrate the plastic. In Pittsburgh I shot a Juggernaut in the visor with standard Parabellum rounds without any effect. I can't say I'm thrilled with the idea of having to rely on hitting such a small target in a firefight in order to bring down an opponent. It was tough enough taking out one Juggernaut that way. Maybe I could handle two if they came at me, but if three or more rushed my position, I'd be lucky if there'd be enough of me left to bury."

"I don't think you'll have to rely on nailing a bull's-eye in the Juggernaut visor next time," Kissinger announced. "I have some new ammunition for you that ought to do the trick."

"No offense, John," Bolan said, "but you told me that last time."

Kissinger climbed off the stool and moved over to another countertop. A set of scales, bullet molds, crimpers and a cabinet stocked with primers, powders and shell casings revealed this to be his "loading section" for the preparation of special ammunition. He handed Bolan a case containing fifty rounds of ammunition.

The Executioner removed a cartridge and immediately recognized it. "Forty-four Magnum," he said. "I thought about using the Desert Eagle. It's a more powerful weapon than the Beretta, but I doubted it would make any difference against the Juggernauts. Some of their opponents used .357 Magnums without any success.''

"But this is special," Kissinger said. "Feel how heavy it is? It's hot loaded at 310 grain."

"I'll be lucky if the barrel doesn't come loose."

"I made some modifications on a Desert Eagle for you," Kissinger said. "A reinforced barrel and frame to handle the bigger grain. It's essential if you're going to be able to fire the projectile with enough velocity to drive it through the Juggernauts' protective gear."

Bolan examined the .44 cartridge. The bullet fitted above the steel casing was made of a gray metal, too hard to be lead. The nose was painted with a blue plastic coat.

"Teflon?" he asked.

"It's a sort of cousin of Teflon," Kissinger answered. "A new synthetic resin developed by the Navy. The bullets are made of a rhodium-tungsten alloy. Guess where I got that idea?"

"The armor-piercing ammunition used by the Juggernauts themselves," Bolan replied. "I've seen those super 10 mm bullets in action. They'll punch through brick, steel and the bulletproof vests worn by the police. Obviously I haven't seen a Juggernaut shoot another Juggernaut, so I'm not sure their ammunition will pierce their own armor."

"They're a ruthless bunch," Brognola commented. "Could be they'd want to make sure none of their people could be taken alive for interrogation. If they found themselves in a tight spot and couldn't take a wounded man with them, I wouldn't be surprised if they chose to kill him instead. That would be hard to do if they couldn't pump a bullet through the guy's armor.''

"I test fired this new ammunition on steel plates twice as thick as those used for the Parabellums," Kissinger said. "These are going to work, Hal."

"Easy to say," the big Fed replied, "but it'll be Striker's head on the line when he goes up against those guys again."

"There's only one way to find out," Bolan said. "Where's that modified Desert Eagle you talked about?"

"Right next door at the indoor firing range," Kissinger replied. "I've got some steel targets set up for you. I'm also working on a modified FAL assault rifle. I know you favor the M-16, but again, the armor-piercing rounds need a grain high enough to propel them with adequate velocity, and we just can't get that with the smaller caliber ammunition used in the M-16. The FAL takes a 7.62 mm cartridge, and I'm confident that'll be big enough to work."

Bolan scooped up the helmet from the counter and tucked it under his arm. Kissinger raised his eyebrows and opened his mouth to say something, but then clearly thought better of it. The Executioner could guess what bothered him: the Juggernaut helmet was their only sample of the advanced armor and Kissinger wanted to protect it.

They moved off to the firing range. Located in the basement level of Stony Man Farm, the range had been designed to test the accuracy of experimental weapons and firearms up to 150 meters. Longer distances were used at the outdoor range, where anything from a submachine gun to a tank could be tested for combat use.

Benches faced the targets of the firing range. Paper silhouettes were the most frequent targets used at the site to help shooters maintain their skill with pistols, but on this occasion, heavy steel plates, similar to what might be used for tank armor, had been placed downrange from a shooter's post.

The modified Desert Eagle waited at that station. The slide was locked back and the magazine-well empty. Two loaded magazines lay on the bench next to the pistol. The Executioner headed downrange to the next aisle. He stacked some sandbags to make an elevated platform and set the headgear on top.

He returned to the benches. Kissinger had acquired Apache earmuff-style protective gear and plastic shooter glasses for all three men. Bolan donned a pair of glasses and hung the Apache muffs around his neck as he inspected the Desert Eagle. He was very familiar with the big Israeli-made pistol, having used it countless times in his missions. Heavy, with a thick barrel and frame, the modified Magnum pistol was even heavier with Kissinger's reinforced metal.

"This is almost as heavy as the .50 Desert Eagle," Bolan remarked, hefting the pistol, muzzle pointed at the ceiling as he moved to the station with the helmet on the range.

"I considered using one," Kissinger said, "but that sucker has enough of a recoil without adding the beefed-up loads for armor-piercing ammunition. You'll feel the extra kick with this baby. If we'd used the .50, you could have ended up with a dislocated shoulder.''

"Okay," Bolan said as he shoved a magazine into the gun, "let's see how she does."

He set the headgear over his ears and thumbed the lever to the pistol slide. The steel snapped shut to chamber the first round and arm the weapon. He gripped the Eagle in a firm two-handed Weaver stance and aimed at the helmet. He inhaled slowly and squeezed the trigger on his exhale. The weapon roared and bucked in his grasp. His arms rode with the recoil, then he brought his fists down swiftly to fire again. The helmet spun on the burlap mound, and he nailed it with a third round before it fell from view behind the sandbags.

"Well," Brognola commented as he removed his ear protectors, "at least it didn't just sit there. Let's find out if the bullets went through it or if they just knocked it over."

Bolan ejected the magazine and cleared the pistol. He set it on the bench, slide locked back once more. He headed downrange to the sandbags, followed by Brognola and Kissinger. He picked up the helmet and showed it to the other men. Three large bullet holes marred the side of the helmet, two near the crown and one at the jawline. Bolan turned the headgear to reveal a trio of larger exit holes.

"They went right through it," Brognola said with a nod of approval. "It looks like you got it right this time, Cowboy."

"Yeah," Kissinger said with a shrug. "Sort of a pity you had to bust up the helmet to make sure it worked, though."

"Don't worry," the Executioner said. "I'll see if I can get you a couple more. Maybe with the heads included."

14

Raymond Stylles handed the metal tray to Andrew Gallow. The renegade inventor peered through the thick lenses of his glasses at the two misshapen pellets, stained with blood and pink-gray tissue. He grimaced and limped across his laboratory to a sink.

"Those are the bullets removed from Dave Holt's head," Stylles said. "Son of a bitch shot him through the visor."

"You already told me," Gallow said as he washed the blood and brain matter from the slugs. "You also said you and others had been shot in the face visors before and neither bullets nor buckshot had penetrated the plastic or even cracked it."

"Not until now," Stylles confirmed. "The bastard used some sort of hot-load ammunition. I got hit in the side of my helmet, and it felt like somebody slapped me hard in the head. It caught me off balance so badly, I tripped over a damn hedge."

"And this mystery gunman didn't appear to be one of Jones's people or a cop?" Gallow asked.

"He was a white guy dressed in black. The late Malachi Jones might have had some whites on his payroll, but the majority of his people were black. Certainly his most trusted personnel were African-

Americans. I guess the gunman might have been a SWAT officer, but I've never heard of one of them acting alone. This one took us on by himself with no backup.''

Gallow held one of the mangled bullets with a pair of tweezers and studied it up close. He grunted and dropped it back onto the tray.

"It's a special armor-piercing 9 mm Parabellum round," he said. "Excellent quality. Whoever came up with this knew his business. Probably made by a military ballistics expert. It doesn't look like anything generally used by the police, unless Detroit has a special section supplying SWAT with advanced armor-piercing bullets. It's not as good as my ammunition, of course. Your mysterious opponent got lucky. If he hadn't shot Holt in the visor, the bullets wouldn't have harmed him.''

"But he did shoot Holt through the visor and the face. One bullet punctured an eye socket, and the other caught him on the bridge of his nose. Our first casualty, Andy. It's not good for the morale of the troops.''

"There's not much we can do about that," Gallow replied with a shrug.

"At least we killed that gunman. We lobbed two grenades through the window of that shoe store. Blew the hell out of it and made sure he wouldn't come out of there alive.''

"That's great, Ray," Gallow said. "But let's not forget you also had to kill Malachi Jones because he was a possible connection to us. St. John wasn't too happy about doing business with a drug dealer... especially a black drug dealer.''

"We've been over this before," Stylles said, his voice weary. "And about confiscating the cocaine and heroin to be sold for funds for our cause. Maybe it's unsavory, but it is profitable. St. John's attitude gets too extreme for my taste."

"I never figured you for a liberal, Ray. Still, most of our people were with St. John when he first started this place, and white supremacy was one of the keystones to building his private army. Their notions of law and order are pretty much the same as ours, even if they do go overboard with 'ethnic purity' and the rest of their hate philosophy."

"We're going to have our hands full establishing a national police force, getting support from the government and the general public, as well as seeking out and destroying criminal elements in our society. We don't need to start a race war on top of that."

"To tell you the truth," Gallow said, "the captain isn't very happy that you've taken it upon yourself to make decisions without informing us first. He thinks it was premature to contact the President, and he didn't like you changing the target from Milwaukee to Detroit without giving us a reason."

"Really? And what do you think, Andy?"

"I'm not a strategist. I'm more a technician, without the background in police or military action that you and Zach can claim. Still, I'm supposed to be one of the leaders here, and I thought my opinion mattered."

"Of course it does," Stylles replied. "Let's find St. John and settle this matter together."

THEY FOUND Zachary St. John in the gym practicing his martial arts. He was sparring with two of his soldier followers, all three dressed in sweatsuits, with leather headguards, codpiece crotch protectors and boxing gloves.

Stylles focused on St. John. The former Airborne Ranger was a hell of a fighter. He faced the troopers in a two-against-one contest, but he still dominated. His gloved fists hammered one opponent with a left jab that forced the man to raise his hands to protect his face, then he quickly altered his left to a hook, hitting his opponent in the side of the head. He followed that up with a right uppercut that lifted the man off his feet and threw him onto his back.

The second adversary moved forward, but St. John weaved out of reach of his flailing fist. He counterattacked with a snap kick to his opponent's unprotected abdomen. Winded, the man staggered backward. St. John advanced, driving a straight right to his breastbone. The blow knocked the trooper off balance, and he fell to the mat as the first man rose once more.

He charged St. John, then suddenly leaped forward, one leg extended in a flying jump kick. It was a flashy, dramatic technique that seemed better suited to a scene from a kung-fu movie than actual combat. The captain sidestepped the attack. His opponent sailed past him, unable to alter his path in midair. St. John moved behind the attacker and pumped a punch to a kidney. The man dropped like a stone and landed on his back.

"What was that, Captain?" Stylles asked as he approached St. John. "Contact karate or kick boxing?"

"It doesn't matter what you call it," St. John replied, his voice even and his breath hardly labored by the exercise, "as long as it works."

"This sort of training really isn't necessary because my body armor makes you impervious to any black belt's punch or kick. The steel gauntlet allows you to strike with greater force than you could ever manage with your bare hands, regardless of how much boxing or karate practice you might do," Gallow said.

"Physical fitness is possibly the most important part of a soldier's training," the captain replied, removing his headgear.

"If you've finished beating up those two, Zach, we need to talk to you," Stylles said.

"I want to talk to you, too," the captain snapped, "and the big question is, what the hell do you think you're doing?"

Stylles shook his head, waiting for the troopers to leave the gym. Once alone, the three leaders of the Juggernauts could converse more freely. They all realized that quarreling in front of their followers would cause the men to doubt their command ability and the success of their movement.

"All right," St. John said, picking up the thread of their conversation. "You called off the mission to the target site in Milwaukee and changed it to an attack on your soul brother buddy in Detroit. One of our men came back in a body bag because of that, Ray."

"I had to make that decision on short notice based on my telephone conversation with Malachi Jones," Stylles explained. "He had just met with some guy who made him an offer to buy a load of cocaine at full-price, then asked if Jones could supply him with heroin, as well. It seemed too suspicious to me. So I told him to terminate this stranger who appeared too good to be for real. I had to take out Jones before he could do anything that might put us at risk.''

''I can't believe you trusted that stupid dealer in the first place,'' the captain said.

''Actually, he wasn't stupid,'' Stylles replied. ''I just had to make sure we'd remain safe. As for the death of David Holt, that was unfortunate, but we knew we'd lose some good men when we started this operation.''

''So much for your body armor making us invincible, Andy,'' St. John said, turning to Gallow.

''The bullets didn't pierce the body armor,'' the inventor insisted. ''The visor gave in after being struck repeatedly by Parabellum hot loads. The late Mr. Holt was too arrogant and presented a clear target at close range. He also disobeyed a direct order when Ray told him to pull back so they could flee the area.''

''If he became overconfident, it was because you gave us all reason to feel that way,'' the captain said. ''I'd say that sense of invulnerability has extended to you, Ray. I'm talking about contacting the President.''

''That was part of our plan all along,'' Stylles replied. ''It seems to have worked to a degree at least. Have you noticed what the President has said about my phone call?''

''To the best of my knowledge he hasn't made any public mention he spoke to you or that he knows anything about our plans for the future of the Juggernauts.''

''Exactly,'' Stylles said with a sly smile. ''That's my point. The President hasn't mentioned it because he hasn't decided whether to accept our offer. Now, we should move on influencing the public to support us, as well."

"I think that might be a bit premature at this point," Gallow said with a frown. "I think we'd better be more concerned with how we're going to continue to finance this operation. Since you decided to terminate Malachi Jones, our revenue from selling confiscated drugs is gone."

"It'll take time to find another source we can deal with to move the drugs," Stylles said. "In the meantime, we need to find another target that will provide us with a lucrative bounty. Let me check our data banks and update the information in the computers to see what's out there."

"I don't like this," St. John admitted. "We're moving too fast. We can't keep hitting target site after target site, throwing plans for attacks just based on information from your computers and virtually no reconnaissance."

"Maybe we can slow our pace," Stylles said, "but first we have to take care of our problem concerning public relations, putting pressure on the government and securing our finances."

"Ray has a point," Gallow cut in. "We know the FBI and other federal agencies are hunting us. They're probably putting together all the clues they can get their hands on. Unfortunately they now have a Juggernaut helmet, although we've been careful not to leave any fingerprints. Since all our equipment was developed independently, nothing can be traced to us, but they'll continue to investigate. They might already have all of us listed as possible suspects because of our field of expertise already on record. I'm sure I'm a suspect, because I've worked on similar projects for the military before.''

"So you don't think we should keep a lower profile?" St. John asked.

"They'll eventually track us down whether we're active or not," Gallow answered. "The only way we can avoid being located and taken down by the government will be if we can convince them to give us legitimate status as a national law-enforcement arm before they come to arrest us as criminals.''

"Criminals?" the captain said and shook his head, clearly appalled at the notion. "How long do you think it'll take them to find us?"

"We'll accomplish our mission and achieve our goals before that happens," Stylles assured him. "Trust me, Zach. I know how these bureaucrats think. I used to work for them. Elected and appointed officials can always be counted on to do what they feel is in their best interests. They'll bend to the will of the public only if they think it will keep them in office so they can enjoy the power they've worked so hard to get. It's a game. You just have to know how to play it if you want to win.''

"Holt is dead and the rest of us are at risk of being arrested," St. John said, "so how can you call this a game?"

"I didn't say it was a civilized game," Stylles replied. "It's as ruthless as hell. If you win, you win big, but if you lose, you lose everything. We're not going to lose.''

15

Kathleen Albert glanced at the papers on her desk and made some notations on them. She had earned her position as an evening news anchor after three decades as a reporter, TV journalist and foreign correspondent in numerous hot spots throughout the world. She was no stranger to handling breaking news stories, but she had never encountered anything quite like this before. She looked up from her notes and faced the familiar red light that signaled the camera was on her.

"We have just been informed of a live satellite broadcast at our studio by a man who claims to represent the Juggernauts," she stated. "This is allegedly the name of the mysterious group of armor-clad gunmen who have been reported in recent crime scenes in Pittsburgh, Los Angeles, Chicago and Detroit. It is important to state that we do not have confirmation that this individual is indeed associated with the Juggernauts, but he is standing by on a satellite broadcast feed that is used by our telecommunications system, and he has appeared to have broken into this system. I've been told we don't know the origin of the broadcast or how this has been accomplished."

A large TV screen at the end of Albert's desk displayed a figure. The metal helmet and tinted visor concealed the person's face, his body-armored torso visible. Behind him hung a white sheet, preventing any telltale evidence that might betray the location of the broadcast.

Kathleen Albert turned to face the monitor. Her expression remained professionally calm as she addressed the armored figure.

"I believe you are violating several FCC regulations by this pirate action," she began.

"Not really," the distorted voice of Raymond Stylles replied. "I don't have time to waste, Ms. Albert. I represent the Juggernauts, as you already stated. I don't intend to reveal my identity at this time, so please don't ask me who I am, where I'm broadcasting from or any other information I obviously have no desire to share."

"Am I allowed to ask why you've decided to make a public statement?" she inquired, an edge creeping into her voice.

"I'm here to clarify the purpose of the Juggernauts," Stylles replied. "We are a special anticrime unit, dedicated to dealing with the most serious and dangerous threats to the United States of America. We locate the centers of extremely violent and well-armed criminal elements and stop them. Since they are ruthless killers, they have been reluctant to surrender. Unfortunately we haven't been able to make arrests, and we've been forced to kill most of them in self-defense."

"What do you mean by self-defense? Our news reports say none of the alleged criminals at any of these sites were placed under arrest by your Juggernauts. In fact a number of police and federal agents were apparently killed by your group.''

"That is incorrect. The law-enforcement personnel were actually killed by the criminals we were attempting to apprehend. Unfortunately they used powerful weapons and explosives. Standard police and federal personnel do not have the protective armor, weapons and training of the Juggernauts.''

"That conflicts with reports made by police investigators, the FBI and the DEA. It also does not explain why none of them know about your organization or why you made no effort to cooperate with them, if you are a lawful unit, as you claim.''

"That is a result of agencies failing to communicate,'' Styles answered. "I'm afraid that's not uncommon when dealing with bureaucracies. Let me assure you this misunderstanding is being corrected, and I'm sure everything will be explained in the future. I also want to assure the law-abiding people of America they have nothing to fear from the Juggernauts. We are only a threat to criminals.''

"Are you suggesting that your organization has been created by the federal government?'' the news anchor challenged. "That you have legal authority to take the sort of action you have been? No federal agency has expressed approval of your Juggernauts. In fact they say they have a nationwide manhunt in progress for you and your group.''

"Of course they'd say that. Those agencies are embarrassed to admit that they've failed to deal with these criminals in the past and we've succeeded. They're trying to discredit us to save their own reputations. We're making this public announcement to reassure the public and to warn the criminals every-where that the Juggernauts are a new kind of national police force. Perhaps if they realize the futility of re-sisting us, they'll surrender in the future and we'll be able to place more of them under arrest, instead of being forced to send them out in body bags.''

"Can you give us the names of any high-ranking officials in the federal government who can support your claims?''

"I believe you'll get a public statement from one or more high-ranking individuals very soon," Styles assured her with a chuckle. "Thank you for your time, Ms. Albert. Goodbye for now.''

The monitor went blank. Albert referred to her notes, finishing her broadcast by recapping the inter-view with the Juggernaut as video footage of the in-cidents in the four major cities appeared on the screen.

JOEL ROSS SHUT OFF the VCR. The President of the United States didn't look at his adviser, but continued to stare at the blank TV screen from his desk in the Oval Office, his expression grim.

"This was broadcast live twenty minutes ago," Ross told him. "It's already being aired on newscasts across the country. You can bet ninety-five percent of the American people will have either seen it, read or heard about it by tomorrow morning.''

"And they haven't been able to track down the origin of the broadcast?" the President asked. "These Juggernauts seem to be able to link up with high-security telecommunications as easily as they can lo-cate criminal bases and carry out destructive raids.''

"Is this the same man you spoke with on Air Force One?" Ross asked.

"That electronic device he uses to distort his voice and alter voiceprints makes it difficult to be sure," the President answered, "but I think it's the same guy."

Joseph Briggs, the President's other adviser, began to pace the floor. Ross glanced over his shoulder at Briggs, as if reluctant to have his eyes off the other man. The President felt that his advisers sometimes held views he found extreme, so more often than not, he decided on a course of action by looking for something in the middle of their recommendations.

"So what do you plan to do, Mr. President?" Briggs inquired, twirling a rubber band around his wrist.

"My immediate reaction is to address the American people in a press conference and declare that these Juggernauts are not, in any way, part of the federal government. That their actions have been completely illegal and they are regarded as renegade criminals and killers, wanted for the murders of law-enforcement officers, among their many crimes."

"I agree with you one hundred percent, sir," Ross stated with a nod. "We need to show that they're nothing but a bunch of vigilante madmen with some funny outfits and assault rifles that should be completely outlawed because they're only used to kill people."

"They use submachine guns," Briggs corrected him, "not those semiautomatic weapons that are referred to as assault rifles by the gun-control people. Submachine guns are already illegal, and the weapons used by the Juggernauts appear to have been manufactured independently. No logos, stamps or serial numbers have been detected in enlarged photographs of their arms. They didn't buy those weapons in a gun shop or even from any black-market dealer. They made the damn things.''

"That's beside the point," Ross insisted. "The President should address the people and publicly denounce the Juggernauts as soon as possible.''

"I said that was my immediate reaction. I didn't say that's what I'd do. First, I'd like to hear what you both think, then I'll talk to the FBI director, the press secretary and maybe a few other people.''

"Well," Briggs began, "I'm opposed to the idea. It's too soon to dismiss these Juggernauts as outlaws who might not serve a genuine role in law enforcement.''

Ross turned to glare at the other adviser as if he thought the man had completely lost his mind. The President also seemed surprised by Briggs's comment.

"Sometimes I wonder if you say things just to see how we'll react," the Man responded. "In this case I can't help but think you aren't really serious.''

"Since when did the U.S. government need a band of professional killers?" Ross asked.

"We've dropped bombs on cities and launched missiles into populated areas," Briggs said with a shrug. "Our military personnel might not be professional killers, but those were actions that definitely killed a lot of people.''

"That's different," Ross insisted. "That's war.''

"Haven't you heard about our war on drugs? The

war on crime? We try to convince the public we're
serious in those 'war' efforts whenever we pass a new
crime legislation that'll cost the taxpayers another bil-
lion dollars or so. The public generally supports this,
too, because they worry about crime. Some of them
have lost family members due to drive-by shootings
and other gang-related violence. They worry about
terrorist bombings like those that happened in New
York and Oklahoma, the sort of thing they used to
think only happened in other countries.''

"We managed to deal with those problems without
creating a death squad to handle them," the President
replied.

"The American public might disagree with you,
sir. Take a look at the targets the Juggernauts picked.
They killed a gang of murderous bank robbers. They
struck at a major crack house in Los Angeles that
everybody in the city knew about—including the police. Local cops didn't take action, because it was
simply too dangerous to launch a raid on the place.''

"That's an outrageous claim and an insult to the
police," Ross declared.

"Then why wasn't any action taken against it before?" Briggs countered. "I'm not saying the cops
are cowards. Over and over we've heard police complain that the gangs and drug dealers are better armed
than they are. We hear it from the DEA. They say
the drug cartels have too much money, too much firepower and they're too powerful to be defeated. Sure,
the DEA and the FBI had those Russian criminals
under surveillance, but they didn't intend to raid them
the night the Juggernauts went in and wiped them out
before that heroin could get on the streets, before it

could be sold to kids and to freaked out junkies who would commit crimes of violence to buy more.''

"The Juggernauts killed several police and agents," the President reminded him.

"We don't know if they started shooting at the Juggernauts first," Briggs replied. "The Juggernauts might have been acting in self-defense."

"Oh, hell," Ross said, "that's absurd!"

"The fact is, the cops and the Feds weren't the targets. They wouldn't have been hurt if they hadn't gotten in the way of the Juggernauts. I'm not saying that what the enforcers did was right—"

"I should say not," the President interrupted him.

"But this sort of thing might not happen again if the Juggernauts have authorization to take action in the future," Briggs insisted. "Whether we like it or not, they've been able to do what no one else has been able to. They already have an impressive Intelligence network, their body armor and weapons are incredible and they sure as hell have guts. Maybe we ought to enlist them and take advantage of their abilities. That way we can keep them from getting out of control."

"They're terrorists and murderers. The United States government doesn't do business with people like that, Joe."

"We don't?" Briggs asked with raised eyebrows. "What about Batista, Somoza, Marcos, the Shah of Iran and a bunch of other nasty people who oppressed and tortured their own people? We supported their governments. We had a lot of them visit this very building as honored guests. When Khrushchev visited the U.S., he was treated like a respected head of state, although he was known as the Butcher of Budapest for slaughter carried out by the Soviet Union against Hungary in the late fifties and early sixties. That's politics, Joel. You do business with all sorts of rotten people when you figure it's in your own best interests to have them on your side rather than against you.''

"Surely you don't agree with this, Mr. President?''

The Man leaned back in his chair and uttered a long sigh. He didn't like what Briggs said, but he realized there was some truth to it. He was opposed to the notion of giving in to the Juggernauts. Still, he had been forced to compromise what he believed to be the right choice more times than he cared to admit since he took the highest executive office in the United States. He hoped this wouldn't prove to be another bitter pill to gag on.

"I've decided to hold off on a press conference until I get a chance to talk to some more people and hear their advice,'' the President announced. "I need to make some phone calls, and I want to do that privately.''

"Yes, sir,'' Ross replied with a nod.

He backed toward the door, still nodding until it changed to a series of bows. The President often found his sycophantic behavior annoying. Briggs might be pragmatic, but at least he left the Oval Office with a simple wave and a snap of the rubber band on his wrist.

The President was eager to contact Stony Man Farm. He hoped Hal Brognola had some encouraging news about the Juggernauts. He could really use some good news, the way things were going.

16

Aaron Kurtzman rolled his wheelchair from the elevator to the Stony Man War Room, a stack of printouts and fax copies on his lap. Hal Brognola had removed a glass case from a special red phone by the table. Kurtzman knew that was the hot line so he knew who the big Fed spoke with even before he heard the man address the person on the other end.

"Yes, Mr. President," Brognola said, "we know about the Juggernaut's broadcast. We tracked the teletransmission to a communications satellite in orbit over the Atlantic. It appears to have been transmitted from another satellite, on a NSA telemetry Signal Intelligence model. Somebody knew the pattern of both orbits and managed to bounce a television broadcast of the SIGINT satellite to the telecommunications system. Sort of a high-tech pool shot, and a pretty slick trick."

"It impressed the hell out of me," Kurtzman muttered.

Brognola cast a glance at him, then turned back to the phone. He listened to the President for a moment, then spoke into the handset again.

"No, we're not sure about the point of origin, but we suspect it was probably done with a radar transmitter system that could be mounted on a truck. Even if we do locate the area of the transmission, the Juggernauts will already be long gone. These guys have brains to go along with their steel-plated armor.''

The big Fed rolled his eyes at something the President said.

''I don't admire them,'' Brognola assured the President, ''but you have to respect an enemy's abilities. You know we've made progress, and we're working on this mission around the clock. I wish I could tell you we'll have this wrapped up in twenty-four hours, but we can't put a specific time limit on it. All I can say is that we're checking out some promising leads and hope to be able to bring this to an end soon.''

The big Fed listened again, then responded. ''A spontaneous press conference? No, I don't think that would be a good idea. The media will obviously question you about the Juggernauts, and there's no need to give them more attention with a special press conference, Mr. President.''

''What's he supposed to say?'' Kurtzman wondered aloud. ''Tell everybody the Juggernauts called him on a secure line to Air Force One? That's like saying these guys are even smarter and more sophisticated than they proved to be by breaking into that telecommunications broadcast.''

Brognola caught Kurtzman's eye and raised a finger to his lips, signaling for silence as he listened to the President. The computer expert shrugged and sorted through his paperwork while he waited for the conversation to end.

''One of your advisers actually said that?'' Brognola asked. ''No way, Mr. President. You can't even consider the possibility of making a deal with these Juggernaut killers. Personally I don't think you should have a press conference or even make an official statement at this time.... Yes, I know you feel that way and I understand the urge to respond immediately to the broadcast. If the media does ask you about the broadcast, you can tell them that it hasn't even been confirmed if it was genuine or a hoax. If they ask your opinion about the Juggernauts' general behavior and raids on criminal outfits, you can tell them that the matter is part of a federal investigation still in progress, so you can't comment at this time."

He listened to the President for another moment, then said, "We do appreciate how important this mission is, and we'll contact you when we have something to tell you. Thank you for the call."

He hung up and turned to Kurtzman, who placed his elbows on the armrests of his chair and locked his fingers.

"What does the President expect us to do that we're not doing already?" he asked.

"He just wants this to be over. The Juggernauts aren't merely a band of vigilantes. They're trying to establish themselves as a national authority by force and coercion. Now they've made their intentions a matter of official public record, and the President is under pressure to decide what to do about them. He contacted us again because he wants us to realize how important this is. He understands we know it already, but right now there isn't much else he can do. His advisers don't seem to be much help."

"And one of them even suggested he consider

making a deal with the Juggernauts?" Kurtzman asked. "Is he serious?"

"Probably," Brognola said with a sigh. "The problem is a large number of people will look at what the Juggernauts offer as a good idea. Send in the shock troops to kick ass seems like a good way to deal with crime. Hell, that's sort of what we do here at the Farm. The big difference is we deal with emergency situations and only use force when it's necessary. We keep a low profile and tight security so we can operate with a small number of people who handle specialized jobs the big Intelligence and law-enforcement agencies can't handle. These Juggernauts want to set themselves up as stormtroopers who will use force, or the threat of force, to bully their way into power. They don't serve the interests of this country. They want the country to put them in charge and let them do what they want, any damn way they want to do it."

"Well," Kurtzman remarked, "they're going to find out that they won't get their way and disappointment can be a real bitch."

"It sounds like you got something."

"I'll explain when Striker gets here."

As if on cue, the elevator doors opened and Bolan emerged. He still carried the modified .44 Magnum Desert Eagle in a hip holster. He had just spent hours at the firing range familiarizing himself with the special armor-piercing, hot-load ammunition developed by Kissinger for the .44 and an FAL assault rifle.

"Got those weapons broken in?" Brognola asked.

"I'd say they're combat ready," Bolan answered,

"although you never know for sure until you actually use a weapon in the field."

"You might get another chance at the Juggernauts sooner than we thought," Kurtzman said. "I had the computers evaluate information about these guys to try to determine where they might strike next. A big concern for them is that they lost their buyer for confiscated drugs when they punched Malachi Jones's ticket to the hereafter. They lost a source of income when that happened, which means they'll probably be looking for a target that can gain them a lot of cash in a hurry. They need a big score, and I think we might have a pretty good idea what it'll be."

He turned to the material on the table. Bolan approached as Kurtzman selected a fax photo and file from his data. The Executioner examined the color picture of a man dressed in a blue suit with a matching tie. His straw-colored hair was professionally styled, as if he were a model, but his wide, pockmarked face, toadlike mouth and small, cruel blue eyes suggested he didn't make a living with his looks.

"That's Lorenzo Chicama," Kurtzman said, "a native of Peru, currently residing in Miami, Florida. He's listed as a visitor assigned to oversee shipments of copper and silver imported from his country to the U.S., but he seems to spend most of his time just hanging out at home and having a good time at various Miami nightclubs and social gatherings. In some circles he's referred to as Daddy Inca.

"Chicama has a pretty nice life-style. He lives in a big house, which could be called a medium-sized mansion—spacious yard, pretty garden, kidney-shaped swimming pool and a stone wall with iron gates for privacy and security in a quiet out-of-the-way area. Not that he owns the house. A good friend, who just happens to be a rich movie star who owns a couple of other big houses in California and Hawaii, and a big luxury apartment in New York City, lets him stay there rent free. I guess he can afford to be generous. The guy can also afford some expensive habits.''

"Would cocaine happen to be among those habits?'' Bolan inquired.

"You've got it," Kurtzman said.

"Chicama could easily smuggle in a hell of a lot of cocaine with legitimate shipments of silver and copper. If he has connections with a respectable metallurgist here in the U.S., customs probably doesn't search the deliveries too hard," Brognola said.

"Looks like that's probably what's going on," Kurtzman confirmed. "Chicama seems to spend a lot of time with folks associated with cocaine use or distribution. DEA surveillance of a number of big dealers in Miami have spotted him time and time again. They had him under surveillance for a while, but they never caught him making a deal, selling coke, using it or carrying a milligram of white powder.''

"But he still lives like a king and has lots of money," Bolan said. "Yet nobody asks how he does this?''

"The guy's popular," Kurtzman answered. "He rides around in a Mercedes he doesn't own. A certain Miami doctor has loaned it to him as long as he's staying in the U.S. He likes to go to nightclubs and restaurants where the owners give him everything on the house or are happy to accept his IOUs. All these people happen to be into cocaine in a big way. Even the money he has isn't really his. People have 'loaned' it to him or asked him to 'hold on to it for them.' He even has documentation to back this up. Written agreements, signed by trusting souls who claim they trust him to pay them back with interest when he returns to Peru.''

''How much money is he currently holding?''

''Probably in the neighborhood of five or six million dollars,'' Kurtzman replied. ''Which is pretty nice when you consider how few expenses the guy has. Since he's not a U.S. citizen, the IRS can't really do much about him. He claims a certain amount of income through import deals and has an accountant in Lima handle his taxes back home.''

''How about getting him deported as an undesirable?'' Brognola asked. ''The Department of Justice helps investigations for the Department of Immigration. There's enough suspicious business here to suggest he's involved in something dirty, even if he hasn't been caught red-handed.''

''Justice isn't eager to get involved in this,'' Kurtzman explained. ''The DEA has backed off, too. Chicama found out they were investigating him, and he got a bunch of lawyers to lay charges of harassment based on racism and prejudice against him because he's from South America. As the DEA didn't have any real proof, they had to stop bird-dogging him.''

''He keeps a multimillion-dollar fortune in cash at that house?'' Bolan asked. ''Not in somebody's borrowed bank account?''

''According to our information, he has most of it

in a wall safe or tucked under his mattress,'' Kurtzman confirmed.

''A tempting target for anybody who knows about it,'' Bolan commented. ''What's he got for security?''

''A pretty standard system with some alarms and a line that signals the police. It would probably take the cops ten minutes to get there if the alarm to them wasn't cut off by whoever decided to hit the place. That wouldn't be hard to do by anybody with access to the blueprints and electrical wiring system. The Juggernauts have been able to get information a hell of a lot more difficult to acquire than that.''

''What kind of personal protection does Daddy Inca have?''

''A twelve-man guard force. All are relatives from Peru—two younger brothers and ten cousins. None of them have criminal records, at least nothing that showed up in a background check. A couple of judges helped to cut some red tape for Chicama's family to legally pack heat. They carry various types of handguns, and keep semiautomatic rifles and shotguns at the mansion as well. It's enough to protect him and his cash from most threats, but I doubt they're prepared for a raid by the Juggernauts.''

''It sounds like a pretty tempting target,'' Brognola mused. ''Lots of money, no Feds or police to speak of—not that the Juggernauts would reject a target due to the presence of law-enforcement officers, but I don't think they want to kill any more cops while they're trying to court public support—and the target is a bad guy involved in drug trafficking. Everybody knows Chicama is dirty, but nobody can touch him. Then along come the Juggernauts and take him out.

A bunch of frustrated Americans will cheer and say it's about time somebody nailed slick suckers like Daddy Inca.''

"There are some other crooked bastards out there with a ton of cash," Kurtzman said, "but none as ripe for the picking as Chicama. Most are under surveillance by local or federal authorities, and a couple of them are better protected than this Peruvian. One or two others might be tempting, but I'd have to say this guy has to be the top choice."

"Let's make sure," Brognola said. "I'll get Leo and his connections with Justice to make sure there is a renewed interest in the other possible targets. Have them hauled in for questioning if there are any grounds. We'll want the Feds to be visible to discourage the Juggernauts. These enforcers have pipelines into federal computer systems, so we'll also want lots of reports flooding in to make sure the Juggernauts know these sites won't be so easy."

"Can Cowboy make more modified weapons for Able Team and Phoenix Force?" Kurtzman asked. "We don't want Mack to have to go up against these armor-plated killers by himself."

"Not on such short notice," Bolan answered. "Besides, we can't risk having our stakeout noticed by the Juggernauts. They'll know it's a trap if they spot anybody stationed near Chicama's place. One man can stay hidden a lot better than a group."

"I don't like you doing this alone," Brognola said with a frown.

"I'm not thrilled with the idea myself," the Executioner admitted, "but it's still the best way to handle it."

"We'll still try to arrange a backup that can be called in if you need them," the big Fed said.

"I've got one more item," Kurtzman announced. "This one came in from Leo in Detroit. While investigating the slaughter of Malachi Jones and his cronies, investigators discovered that Jones managed to switch on a tape recorder before the Juggernauts killed him. On it, he referred to one of his assassins as Webster. They even had a brief conversation before Jones's skull was rearranged by a 10 mm slug. Webster apologized for having to kill Jones. Wasn't that considerate?"

"Do they have enough for a decent voiceprint?" Bolan asked.

"The voice was muffled," Kurtzman answered. "He was probably wearing a helmet at the time. So they're not sure about a voiceprint, and there are a limited number of them on file anyway. The name Webster is almost certainly a cover name."

"Wasn't there a former FBI director named Webster?" Bolan inquired.

"William Webster was Bureau director back in the late 1970s," Kurtzman answered, displaying his brain was as impressive a source of information as any of his computers. "You think the guy is FBI or a former Fed? Well, the Juggernauts sure know how to tap into government data sources, current intel and communications under federal regulation."

"You think this Juggernaut has decided to take an identity that would satisfy some sense of nostalgia for his old days in the Bureau? So he chooses his former boss's name?" Brognola said. "That might be stretching it, Striker. Maybe if he used the cover name of Hoover or Sessions, I'd be more inclined to think there might be a connection.''

''Hell,'' Kurtzman growled, ''these Juggernauts are a crazy bunch, so we don't know what might inspire them. They want to establish themselves as a sort of elite national police force. Maybe an ex-Fed would find that appealing. Especially if he had a personality that combined a desire for law and order under an iron fist with a drive for personal power and authority. That kind of thing might have gotten him bounced out of the FBI or some other outfit.''

''We could be barking up the wrong speculative tree altogether,'' Brognola said. ''It won't make much difference if the Juggernauts are former FBI, or whatever, who want to make the world safe, when Striker encounters them in the field again. Maybe the new ammunition Cowboy came up with can penetrate Juggernaut armor, but you won't have any bulletproof vest that can protect you from those supercharged 10 mm rounds they use, either.''

''Yeah,'' Bolan said, ''I'm aware of that. I also know from past experience their armor-piercing ammunition can punch right through a lot of materials one might use for cover in a firefight. I'll just have to make sure I don't get shot.''

17

It has been said that money couldn't buy happiness, but it could certainly keep misery at a distance. Lorenzo Chicama appeared to be quite happy as he frolicked in a whirlpool tub with two young women, a stereo system providing background music. Chinese lanterns hung from wires above the tub, and a pool-side tray held champagne. They paid no attention to the two gun-toting men who patroled the larger kidney-shaped pool nearby.

The Executioner lay on his belly less than three hundred yards away, observing the mansion through a Starlight scope. He swept his instrument across the gates, stone walls and armed guards around the site— adequate protection from anything less than a major assault by a company of well-armed troops, or half a dozen Juggernauts.

Bolan had been in position for three hours, but time dragged under the conditions of his watch. He was dressed in a combat blacksuit, with the modified .44 Magnum Desert Eagle in a hip holster and three M-26 fragmentation grenades on his belt. He carried spare magazines for the big pistol, as well as the FAL assault rifle that lay beside him. He'd included night-vision goggles, a Ka-bar combat knife and two garrotes. Also on hand was a radio transceiver. The compact unit would keep him in touch with Able Team, posted one and one-half miles from his position, allowing him to communicate with them by means of the earplug and throat mike he wore. They would provide backup in an emergency, although Bolan knew he would be reluctant to do so because Schwarz, Blancanales and Lyons weren't armed with Kissinger's special armor-piercing ammunition and modified weapons. He would call on his fellow Stony Man warriors only if it came down to the wire.

The soldier did another survey of the big house. He realized he might be stuck at his post until dawn without any sign of the Juggernauts. Then, too, the armor-plated vigilantes might have picked a different target, or decided to lie low for a while. They might even decide to attack Chicama or some other target in daylight, although all their previous raids had been launched at night.

Bolan rolled onto his side to stretch a cramped muscle. A flash of light by the driveway to the mansion suddenly drew his attention back to the site. Raising the Starlight scope, he peered down at the two vans with bulky frames and tinted glass that rolled to the front gate, as four guards assembled by the entrance to see who the late-night callers might be.

The Executioner instantly recognized the Juggernaut-style armored vehicles. He didn't need more evidence that the enemy had arrived. Reaching for the FAL assault rifle, he left his cover and sprinted to his Ford Taurus, parked behind a row of bushes and laced with loose tree branches for additional camouflage.

As he slid behind the steering wheel, he heard the bellow of explosions in the distance and guessed that the Juggernauts had probably blown the gates with grenades.

Turning on the ignition, he steered the car around the bushes and rolled downhill to the road. Although it branched off from the busy Palmetto Expressway to greater Miami, the side road was seldom traveled and Bolan encountered no traffic at that hour. He hit the road and accelerated as he headed for Chicama's home. He didn't turn on the headlights but relied on his night-vision goggles to allow him to see the road in the dark.

Then the Executioner heard gunfire. The hill blocked his view of the house, but he knew Chicama's goons wouldn't last long against the Juggernauts. Two vehicles had arrived at the mansion, which meant the attack force was probably twice as large as the previous Juggernaut raids. It would mean taking on eight or ten armor-plated opponents instead of four or five as before.

He took a bend in the road and caught sight of the outline of the estate. Lights popped on rapidly at the site, as if a mob of paparazzis had converged on the home of a celebrity. The sounds of battle grew louder as the Taurus reached the driveway. The Executioner parked at the shoulder and grabbed his rifle. Kissinger's superammunition was about to get the ultimate test in the field, Bolan thought, aware that his life depended on whether the armor-mpiercing rounds proved effective against the Juggernauts.

Twin columns of poplars flanked the driveway. Bolan used the slender trees for cover as he advanced on foot, the gloom of night and the surrounding shadows supplying extra concealment.

He came upon the vans parked in front of the mangled metal that had formerly been iron gates. The bloodied remains of Daddy Inca's thugs littered the area. A single armed figure clad in gray body armor and helmet stood guard by the vehicles, his attention focused on the big house and the battle that continued to rage inside the property. Apparently the sentry was more interested in the conflict between his comrades and the hoods than concerned with any threat from the road.

The Executioner knew he had to take advantage of the situation. Raising the buttstock of the FAL to his shoulder, he aimed at the broad backplate of the Juggernaut. Bolan didn't like taking out an opponent in this manner. To kill a man who was facing you—coming at you to cause death or injury—was clear self-defense. Shooting a man from behind, without warning, was something different.

But Bolan was at war. The Juggernauts had started the nation-wide conflict, and they had to be stopped. He couldn't take chances with an enemy as ruthless and dangerous as the armor-clad killers. Setting the sights of the rifle at the back of the sentry's helmet, he squeezed the trigger.

The FAL roared and kicked back into his shoulder. The Juggernaut's head jerked violently to the side from the impact of the 7.62 mm round. The Executioner saw the bullet hole in the helmet even before the sentry collapsed to the ground.

Bolan moved forward to the fallen form and glanced at the body. An exit hole in the helmet left no doubt that the modified bullet had pierced the Juggernaut's skull. The dead vigilante didn't appear human—just a lump of curious junk, a robot that had toppled after the Off switch had been pressed.

Movement at the wide steps to the front of the house caught the soldier's attention. Two Juggernauts had emerged, each carrying a canvas bag in one gloved hand and a 10 mm submachine gun in the other. Alive and mobile, the armored opponents presented a very different and dangerous image. Bolan flicked the fire selector switch on the rifle from semi- to full-automatic as the pair approached.

"Watch out!" yelled a voice muffled by a helmet.

The Juggernaut had spotted Bolan. As he dropped his bag to grab the subgun with both hands, the Executioner aimed his weapon. He had a second to notice the other Juggernaut didn't appear alarmed, probably confident his body armor would protect him. Bolan concentrated on the enemy about to bring his subgun into play and triggered a 3-round burst. A triangle of bullet holes in the opponent's breastplate marked Bolan's accuracy. The weapon slipped from gloved fingers as the Juggernaut stumbled backward, then crashed to the ground.

Astonished at seeing a comrade in supposedly invincible armor go down, the second Juggernaut stood frozen for a moment. Then he cast aside his bag and grabbed his weapon, as he tried to make for the shelter of a marble statue by an outdoor fountain. The body armor wasn't designed for speed, and the gunman's efforts were slow and clumsy. Bolan tracked him, drilling him with another trio of metal-piercing projectiles. The man was knocked off balance from the force of the bullets, and he slammed into the statue, snapping off a marble arm. The Juggernaut collapsed to the ground, the amputated stone arm sticking up incongruously from beneath his own arm.

Bolan advanced. He stepped across the smashed iron gates to enter the spacious grounds, complete with rose gardens, ornate fountains and more marble figures. More gray armored enforcers appeared at the front entrance to the mansion. They saw their slain comrades and scanned the area for the cause. The soldier sprinted for cover by a pair of stone nymphs, then raised his FAL and opened fire.

The enemy returned fire. The 10 mm hot loads pelted the area around the Executioner, exploding the marble head of a nymph and showering him with stone fragments. Bolan responded immediately, more to impair their marksmanship than to bring down an opponent from that distance.

The Juggernauts marched toward the soldier's position, submachine guns blasting. Bolan ducked his head around the edge of the statue to get a fix on where the enemy was and how many he had to deal with. Three armored killers had moved within twenty yards of him. If they could keep him pinned down, the trio could separate and catch him in a cross fire at close range. They might also try to use grenades, Bolan realized. However, he, too, carried M-26 fraggers, and he decided to use the explosives before the killers chose that option.

The Executioner yanked the pin from a grenade and popped the spoon. Gripping the M-26 in one hand, he fired the rifle with the other, the barrel jammed against the side of the statue. Using his rifle fire to discourage his opponents from closing in or fanning out, Bolan hurled the grenade at the enemy.

He ducked behind the marble figures as the bomb exploded. The force of the blast knocked off chunks of white marble, and dust rained onto Bolan's back and shoulders. He shook off the debris and swung around what remained of the statues.

One Juggernaut lay on his back, his breastplate smashed in like a dented tin can. The man's helmet was gone, and so was most of his face. Another vigilante lay sprawled on the ground, his arm ripped off at the shoulder. The third Juggernaut was on his hands and knees. He had lost his submachine gun and although stunned by the explosion, he didn't appear to be mortally wounded.

Yet another armored figure emerged from the house, a sack of loot slung over a shoulder and a submachine gun held in his hand. The dazed Juggernaut began to rise, but Bolan swung his FAL toward the newest and potentially more serious threat. He snap aimed for the man at the head of the stairs and squeezed the trigger. Nothing happened. He glanced at the open chamber port and realized he had exhausted his ammunition.

The Juggernaut who had been knocked down by the explosion was on his feet, and he realized Bolan's rifle was empty. He bellowed and charged, fists balled, prepared to beat his adversary to death with his steel gauntlets. The hardman on the stairs took in the scene below and discarded his booty to grip his weapon with both hands. He descended the stone steps, his subgun aimed at Bolan, but held his fire as his comrade launched himself at the Executioner.

Bolan didn't have time to reload the FAL or draw the Desert Eagle from hip leather. He quickly adjusted his hold on the rifle, gripping the barrel and frame. The fist-wielding Juggernaut drew closer and threw a wild right at the Executioner. Bolan parried the attack by bringing the rifle's steel barrel to the outside of his attacker's forearm, turning the shaft in a circular motion and slipping it inside the crook of the man's elbow.

The Executioner stepped to the right of his opponent and shoved the FAL higher in a rapid motion. The startled Juggernaut suddenly found his arm twisted back in a hammerlock, secured by the rifle's barrel. Despite the fancy body armor, the joints inside remained human, and Bolan had gotten control of his adversary's arm. He gripped the barrel near the muzzle with one hand to hold the FAL like a bar and increased the pressure on the limb trapped behind the Juggernaut's back.

The man on the stairs advanced as fast as his armor would allow, and tried to move into position to get a clear shot at Bolan. He aimed his subgun and the soldier turned sharply, forcing the captive Juggernaut to move with him. The submachine gun snarled and Bolan felt his prisoner convulse. The gunman had shot his fellow Juggernaut in the breastplate with at least three 10 mm armor-piercing rounds.

Swiftly Bolan drew his .44 Magnum with one hand as he shoved the dying hardman toward his comrade with the other. The Executioner dropped to one knee and fired the big pistol the instant he saw the gunman's metal torso. The .44 roared and the special Magnum load hit the Juggernaut in the center of his breastplate. The powerful round drove back his adversary, and Bolan shot him again with a .44 left of center. The Juggernaut went down hard, his body twitching inside the metal shell until he lay still.

The roar of a car engine penetrated Bolan's ears over the ringing aftereffects of the battle. Two bright white lights appeared, advancing rapidly. Bolan hit the ground and rolled away from the onrushing vehicle, coming up in a kneeling stance as he saw a black Mercedes bolt for the driveway.

The Executioner fired at the fleeing vehicle. The .44 Magnum round burst the trunk latch and it popped open, but the Mercedes kept on going. Suddenly a metal sphere was hurled from the car's window, landing by the abandoned vans. Bolan ducked just before the grenade exploded. The blast tore apart one van, igniting the fuel tank. Burning wreckage quickly covered the driveway, and soon the second van was shrouded in flaming gasoline.

Bolan had lost sight of the Mercedes, and he realized that by the time he got past the fiery debris to reach the Ford Taurus, the escaping vehicle would be long gone. He knew he could radio Able Team to try to cut off the Mercedes, but as he didn't know which direction the big black car had taken, their odds of finding it would be no higher.

"Well," Bolan said to himself as he glanced about the combat zone, "most of them didn't get away this time. The rest just got a reprieve."

18

John Kissinger raised a muscular arm, his hand, wrist and forearm covered by a Juggernaut's gauntlet. He clenched his gloved fist and swung it like a hammer into a thick pine board set between a pair of saw-horses. Wood cracked and the board snapped in the middle.

"An instant karate expert," Hal Brognola commented.

Mack Bolan looked on as Kissinger removed the gauntlet and handed it to Brognola.

"This thing turns your hand into a steel war club," Kissinger said. "This Juggernaut body armor is pretty impressive. Their submachine guns aren't shabby, either. Good craftsmanship went into the design of those weapons, although they are heavy, what with all the reinforcement needed to handle those superhot 10 mm rounds, and the rate of fire is slow. Still, the Juggernauts have a decent firearm. The 10 mm is a nice touch. Haven't I said that caliber has the potential to be the top choice in the future?"

"I think we've heard you mention that before," Brognola replied in a weary tone, "but Striker didn't bring this stuff back from Miami so you could start a Juggernaut fan club. We want you to help us take out these clowns.''

''Mack took out six or seven of them using the ammo I made for the Desert Eagle and the FAL,'' Kissinger countered, ''so I am doing my job.''

''Yeah,'' Bolan confirmed. ''They worked just fine.''

The telephone rang in Kissinger's workshop, and he picked up the receiver. He listened for a moment, said, ''I'll tell them,'' and hung up.

''That was Aaron,'' he announced. ''Says he's got something for you, and he'll meet you two in the War Room.''

Bolan and Brognola headed for the Farm's War Room, where Aaron Kurtzman was already waiting for them. He had another stack of papers and faxes in front of him. Brognola stuck an unlit cigar into his mouth and slumped into his chair.

''First,'' Kurtzman began, ''we've got some reports from the Miami police. Quite a slaughter at that Chicama's place. Of course, you already know the Juggernauts killed everybody there—Daddy Inca, his bodyguards and a couple of high-priced ladies. Add on the seven Juggernauts Striker took out, and the total comes to twenty-two. That's a lot of body bags for one place.''

''What do the police think happened?'' the big Fed asked, chewing on his cigar.

''They think it was about drugs, one way or the other. They found sacks filled with money and figured it was an attempted rip-off. They seem to think the Juggernauts and Chicama's people killed each other.''

"Is that what they're telling the media?" Brognola asked.

"The Miami cops are in touch with the FBI and Justice. They know this is a concern for the federal government and that the Juggernauts have struck all over the nation. The police have agreed to keep a lid on the Juggernauts' involvement for the next twenty-four hours to give the Feds time to consider if this is a matter of national security and how to handle it."

"That's quite a stack of information you've got there," Bolan said, nodding at Kurtzman's files. "Is it all police reports, or is there anything more useful in there?"

"Glad you asked," Kurtzman replied as he sorted through his papers and selected several faxes. "We've got positive ID's on five of the dead Juggernauts in Miami. The other two were either mangled by explosions or burned pretty bad. The FBI is still working on them to be sure."

"Good," Brognola said. "Now we get to find out what kind of nut cases would join a terrorist outfit, dress up in body armor and run around the country carrying out murder, mayhem and attempted blackmail of the U.S. government."

"The answer isn't a big surprise," Kurtzman said. "Three of these guys had served time for criminal assault. One got two years for manslaughter in Maryland. He beat a guy to death with an ax handle in a parking lot outside a bar in Baltimore. The other two Juggernauts were also once charged in assault cases, but they managed to plea-bargain down to misdemeanors."

"All assault cases?" Bolan asked. "No robbery, burglary or fraud?"

"None. There's an interesting trait all these guys seemed to have had in common. Just about all of them seemed to have gotten into trouble over hate crimes with racial motives. One guy had participated in beating up a Vietnamese immigrant, and one real macho piece of work punched out a black guy. The one who beat another guy to death said he did it because the fella followed him outside to continue an argument they'd had in the bar over capital punishment. Witnesses said he called the man he would later kill a 'goddamn bleeding heart liberal who deserved a good ass-kicking,' or words to that effect."

"So these jerks were up-right citizens, except for nasty tendencies like attacking minorities and killing liberals who disagreed with their views," Brognola growled.

"I imagine that's how they thought of themselves," Kurtzman replied. "It gets better. Four of these characters were veterans of the United States Army and happened to serve under the same company commander by the name of Captain Zachary St. John. This same captain resigned his commission and left the service after several accusations of racism and beating the hell out of an enlisted man because he caught the soldier smoking some grass in a latrine."

"You seem to think St. John is still connected to these other misfits," Bolan remarked.

"That's because he is," Kurtzman stated. "It turns out that St. John came from a rather rich family in Georgia who left him a few million dollars, a nice chain of businesses and some pretty valuable property. He sold all the businesses and the property to acquire more money before he bought some land not far from Atlanta. There he set up his own private training camp. Guess who he invited to join him?''

"Some of his favorite fellow bigots from the Army?"

"Right. The FBI, Justice and BATF all took an interest in St. John's group awhile back, but they didn't poke too hard because St. John came from a well-to-do, respectable family and he claimed his camp was training professional bodyguards. Still, the Feds kept some of the results of their investigations on record. This included the names of known members of St. John's group at the time."

"And the dead Juggernauts are among them?" Brognola asked.

"Everybody except the killer who served time for manslaughter," Kurtzman answered. "I suspect he might have been there, too, using an assumed name. It wouldn't surprise me if the other two corpses turn out to be his pals after the FBI manages to ID them."

"We might have hit the mother lode," Bolan remarked.

"Yeah," Brognola agreed, "but we still don't know how St. John came up with this advanced body armor or managed to do all the fancy computer links and data gathering. That requires considerable expertise and knowledge about federal Intelligence networks. Does his background or that of any of his comrades suggest that they'd be capable of anything this sophisticated?"

"Not that I've found," Kurtzman replied. "St. John was an Airborne Ranger—lots of commando skills, an expert with an M-16 rifle, grenades, pistol, M-60 machine gun. He has a second dan black belt in karate and is big on fitness and parachuting. He's certainly not an engineer, inventor or computer whiz. Of course, who knows what a man might learn on his own. But it's more likely he brought in some people with those skills.''

''I'll let you know what I find when I check out the place,'' Bolan announced as he consulted his wristwatch. ''Do you figure Grimaldi can be ready to fly me out of here within an hour? I want to get to Georgia as fast as possible.''

''That might be rushing it, Striker,'' Brognola said. ''We can get you down there, but Able Team is still in Miami, so I can't promise you we'll have them there for backup.''

''Jack can work backup if I need it,'' Bolan replied. ''We don't have time to waste, Hal. The Juggernauts aren't stupid. They had to leave their dead cohorts behind, so they'll know they can be identified and investigated. They'll be sure to haul out if they suspect we've located their base.''

''I don't like the idea of your going into a site crawling with armor-plated lunatics. Who knows how many of them are at that place.''

''The number of St. John's followers was estimated to be about twenty when the Feds investigated him,'' Kurtzman stated. ''There might be a few more or a few less by now, but we know that they're definitely minus seven of their members.''

''Minus eight,'' Bolan said. ''Don't forget the one in Detroit. Look, Hal. I'll try to go in with a soft probe to confirm that it is the Juggernauts' headquarters. We can figure out how to handle them then, and whether to call in the FBI, BATF or the National Guard. If nothing else, I want to find out if those guys have any women or children at that camp so we can do our best to avoid injuring them.''

"Okay," Brognola agreed reluctantly. "I'll get Leo down there, too, in case we need to smooth over things with the local police or Feds stationed in the Atlanta area. Be careful, Striker. These Juggernauts have already proved they're crazy and dangerous as hell. If they feel cornered, they'll be even worse."

"I'll bear that in mind," the Executioner said dryly.

19

Zachary St. John had been forced to make concessions to the state authorities. Plans to set up an electrified fence around the compound, even with signs posted, were vetoed because it was considered a potential risk to citizens, especially children too young to understand warning signs.

He'd also had to alter training exercises that used live ammunition and explosives that were declared too hazardous to public safety. A roving patrol of armed guards was permitted to drive around inside the area, but not outside the fence. Several surveillance cameras were posted on the property as well as some motion detectors. Two sentries were on duty by the gated entrance.

Bolan had infiltrated places with much tighter security. He dealt with the human security simply by avoiding them, waiting for the roving patrol to pass by the part of the fence he had selected for his entrance. Spotting the location of the cameras and motion detectors wasn't difficult, as they were covered with plastic to protect them from the weather.

With the aid of an entrenching tool, the Executioner dug a shallow hole at the base of the fence large enough to crawl through. Using the surrounding bushes and trees for concealment he crawled for at least three hundred yards, avoiding detection from the roving patrol and the motion detectors.

His method of entry was successful, but it had also been time-consuming, so that darkness had descended before he approached the buildings at the center of the compound. Dressed in his blacksuit, the Executioner advanced, armed with the Beretta 93-R pistol—sheathed in a special holster designed to accommodate a sound suppressor—and the modified Desert Eagle, loaded with the special .44 Magnum rounds. He also carried a pack of lock picks, a compact pocket camera and a sound-magnification device. Three fragmentation grenades, a smoke grenade canister, and the Ka-bar fighting knife and garrotes rounded out his arsenal.

The heart of the compound was a typical paramilitary setup. Two long single-story structures appeared to be billets for the troops. The motor pool consisted of two pickup trucks, a pair of Jeeps and a two-and-one-half-ton military-style transport truck. A large house probably functioned as the headquarters.

The only structure that seemed to be out of place was a barn, painted red from roof to base. There were no farm animals, or evidence of any agricultural activity at the camp.

Bolan didn't waste time speculating about the barn. Instead, he watched as several men, dressed in camouflage fatigues and wearing boots, labored by the billets and the rear of the house. They hauled crates, loading the cargo onto the back of the big truck. If they were getting ready to flee, they certainly seemed to be taking their time packing their gear. The population at the camp didn't seem very large. If there were less than a dozen men at the site, that would be fine with Bolan. The fewer eyes to see him and the fewer opponents to contend with, the better.

The Executioner stealthily circled the base, using available cover. The men in paramilitary garb didn't seem alert to a possible threat and concentrated on their chores. Bolan didn't see or hear evidence of women or children at the compound. If violence erupted, he wouldn't have to worry about innocent bystanders.

He approached the house from the east wing and searched for an entrance. He found one—an open window with only a screen to deal with. There didn't seem to be any wires to an alarm as he carefully probed the edges of the screen with a lock pick. Removing the barrier, he climbed into the room. In the gloom, he could just make out a bed, a wall locker and a small desk.

Moving to the door, he carefully opened it just enough to peer into the corridor. It was empty and he opened the door wider. The narrow hallway was almost bare. Tube lights on the ceiling illuminated drab gray walls and a black-and-red checkerboard tiled floor. He stepped into the corridor and edged his way toward the rear of the building.

Voices at the end of the corridor caused him to halt, his back pressed against the wall. He heard two men talking, their voices growing clearer as they drew closer. Silently he slid the Beretta from shoulder leather.

"Zach isn't going to like this idea," a voice declared. "He's already furious that seven of the men didn't come back from Miami. He said he was lucky to get out of there alive.''

"None of us guessed anyone would have ammunition that could pierce your body armor,'' the other man replied. "Hell, Andy, I'm as shocked as you and St. John are that this happened. The fact is, it did, and now we have to come up with a new plan of action, pronto.''

"But robbing armored cars is pretty contrary to what we intended to do with the Juggernauts. Have you lost sight of our reason for starting this in the first place?''

"No, I'm just being practical. We still need a lot of cash to continue our operations. Somehow, someone second-guessed us in Miami. We have to use a tactic they won't expect, and they won't expect us to rob armored cars instead of dope dealers.''

"How can we get the public to support us as a national police force, Ray? We're becoming common thieves who aren't even choosing criminals as our targets.''

"We'll disguise our armor and use a different type of helmet. Something smaller that can be concealed under a stocking mask. No one will know the Juggernauts are responsible.''

The two men came into view. Bolan remained motionless as the pair stood at the end of the hallway, less than three yards from his position. One guy was tall, blond and athletic. The other wore a loose-fitting lab coat and thick glasses. He carried an instrument that resembled a remote-control unit.

Suddenly the blond man turned his head and his gaze locked on Bolan. His eyes widened, and he reached for the pistol in a side-draw holster on his belt. The Executioner had the muzzle of his Beretta fixed on the man before he could unleather his weapon.

"Make a move or raise your voices, and you're dead," Bolan warned. "Face the wall and spread them."

"What the hell are you doing here?" Raymond Stylles began. "I thought I killed you when I blew up that shoe store in Detroit."

"Wrong, but then you guys have been wrong about a lot of things," the Executioner replied.

Andrew Gallow held the remote-control unit low in his hand and suddenly depressed a button with his thumb. Without warning, a fiery pain shot through Bolan's feet, into his legs and up into his body. His arms convulsed out of control, and the Beretta flew from his grasp. His muscles contracted, and a black mist began to descend upon him. Then all his senses seemed to shut down. He felt nothing when he fell to the floor.

"HE'S COMING AROUND," a voice said as if from the end of a dark tunnel.

As Bolan regained consciousness, the cobwebs of confusion began to disappear from his mind. His body felt numb, but he didn't seem to be injured. He tested his limbs before he tried to open his eyes. His legs were sprawled in front of him on the floor, and he moved one foot, then the other. Nothing seemed to be broken.

His arms didn't respond as well. They were behind him, and he realized he was handcuffed. Without warning, a hard blow struck the side of his face, sending his head rocking. He slitted his eyes, but his vision was blurred so that the figure appeared to be shrouded in a gray fog.

"Easy, Captain," a voice urged. "You'll knock him out again before he comes fully to."

The fog lifted. Bolan recognized the features of Zachary St. John from the file photographs, but the former Airborne Ranger's face hadn't burned with hatred in those pictures. The man who glared down at Bolan appeared ready and willing to tear his head off with his bare hands.

Bolan was relieved when St. John stepped back, rising to his full height. Dressed in Army fatigues, paratrooper boots and a holstered side arm, he looked every inch the military man. His companion in the lab coat stood with his arms folded across his narrow chest, peering down at Bolan through his thick glasses, as if examining a specimen under a microscope. A third figure lurked behind the pair. He sported full body armor. The only thing missing was his helmet.

As the Juggernaut leaned forward, the Executioner recognized him as the second guy he had encountered in the corridor. A cruel smile slithered across Raymond Stylles's lips as he nodded at Bolan.

"Can you talk?" he asked. "Didn't get your vocal cords shocked into paralysis, did you?"

"You're probably wondering what happened," the man in the lab coat said.

"Yeah," Bolan admitted, his tongue thick in his dry mouth. "I thought I had the drop on you two."

"Not after I used this," Gallow announced as he

waved his remote-control unit. "I activated a security system in the floor. You were hit by at least seventy thousand volts. Nonlethal electricity, no amps. Otherwise you would have been burned to a crisp."

"Electricity? But my boots have rubber soles."

"It doesn't matter," the scientist replied. "The electrodes in the floor extend electric currents similar to certain types of handheld stun guns on the market. Your feet were caught in a crisscross of electrical currents."

"Clever," Bolan had to admit. "But why did you have it installed in your own headquarters? Are you worried about a possible mutiny by your troops?"

"You'd better worry about yourself," St. John snapped.

"As you can tell, Zach is upset with you," Stylles commented. "He says you took out a number of his men in Miami. Now, that fascinates me because I saw you in Detroit. So who the hell are you, some crazy lone wolf chasing after us all by yourself?"

"Do you think I'm the only one who knows about your base?" Bolan challenged. He even managed a faint smile. "So you just relax and figure you're safe. After all, you guys are smarter than everybody else, anyway. That's been your attitude from the start."

"You don't understand what we're trying to accomplish," Gallow said. "Crime is out of control in this country. We can establish a national police force that can deal with the worst, most dangerous criminal elements in society. We've proved that already."

"The only thing you've proved is that your Juggernauts can break down doors and kill a lot of people, including law-enforcement officers trying to do their job," Bolan replied.

"We didn't plan that to happen," St. John insisted. "It had to be done because they got in the way."

"Got in your way?" Bolan said. "Who else will have to die when they 'get in your way'? Anyone who objects to your tactics? Anybody who believes stormtroopers aren't the way to deal with crime? Anybody who thinks giving up our rights and freedom is too high a price to be 'safe' under a police-state dictatorship?"

"That's quite a speech," Stylles said, sneering. "So we should just let the savages run free? Let them tear America apart, poisoning it with drugs and terrorizing it with threats of gang violence?"

"I don't think murderers and terrorists should be allowed to prey on innocent people," Bolan replied. "And that includes your Juggernauts. Use whatever excuse you want to justify your actions, but you're just a bunch of armor-plated thugs with a gangster mentality who want permission to carry out any sort of brutality against anyone you choose."

"This debate isn't accomplishing anything," Stylles said. "I'm going to search the area with some troops to see if you have any reinforcements hiding out there. It's hard to imagine anyone would come against us alone, although you seem to have tried it before. Still, you couldn't have managed all this by yourself."

"While Stylles is looking for your friends," St. John said, "I'm going to interrogate you. That is going to be a pleasure. I'm looking forward to making you talk."

"It's really too bad," Gallow said. "A man with such obvious courage and skill should be on our side. I'm actually sorry it has to end like this."

"Don't worry, it's not over yet," the Executioner replied.

"Try not to kill him before he talks," Stylles told St. John. "There's a lot we need to know, such as how he showed up at our target sites and how he came up with ammunition that can pierce our armor."

"Rest assured, he'll tell us everything he knows," St. John answered. "Hallaron and I know how to make people talk."

"Too bad we don't have truth serum," Gallow commented. "I think it would be more reliable than trying to beat the truth out of this man."

"But not nearly as satisfying."

Stylles left the room. Gallow prepared to follow, but St. John stopped him. The captain drew a .45 Colt from his hip holster and handed it to the scientist, saying "Standard procedure for interrogation. The bastard won't get an opportunity to get his hands on this weapon, but let's not take any chances."

Gallow accepted the pistol and departed. The Executioner glanced around the room. It seemed to do duty as a storage area and was stocked with camping equipment, tents and various tools. Apparently the compound didn't have a cell block, so they had to improvise.

A stocky man with a heavy brow entered the room. He hefted a large armchair, and a length of rope was coiled around his shoulder. He set the chair in the center of the room, tossed the rope onto the seat and closed the door.

"This is Sergeant Hallaron," St. John announced. "He has a special talent for inflicting pain, and a very strong stomach to go with it."

Hallaron turned to Bolan and waved a Ka-bar knife at him. A smile appeared on his wide face as he approached the Executioner.

"Do you recognize this?" he asked. "This is your own knife, and I'm going to use it on you. Ironic, isn't it?"

"And we brought you a chair," St. John added, patting the armrest. "Have a seat. You're in for a long, hard night."

20

The enforcers had confiscated Bolan's weapons while he'd been unconscious, but they hadn't taken his belt or his boots. Stealthily, while his captors were busy getting organized, his fingers probed inside the belt at the small of his back. They closed around the handcuff key in the hidden compartment in the leather, and he carefully eased it out.

Avoiding as much movement of shoulders or arms as possible, he inserted the key into the steel cuff attached to his left wrist. Most handcuffs were universal in design, taking a standard key. Bolan hoped the Juggernauts hadn't used some unusual model that required a different type of key.

"You guys must realize this scheme is down the drain," he said, more to distract his captors and stall for time than with any hope of changing their minds. "If you cooperate, you might be able to turn state's evidence—"

"Shut up!" St. John barked. "We're not about to betray our cause!"

"Hell, sir," Hallaron said with a chuckle, "let him whine. It'll be sort of fun to listen to him go from being reasonable to crying like a goddamn baby."

The renegade sergeant leaned over Bolan and

pointed the blade of the knife at his face, inches from his left eye.

"Get up, you piece of dirt!" Hallaron ordered.

Bolan nodded, starting to get to his feet as Hallaron moved back slightly. In the same instant, the Executioner swung his left arm forward, the unlocked handcuffs in his fist. Before the sergeant could react, Bolan had snapped the steel bracelet onto the man's knife wrist.

Even as his right arm rose, delivering an upper-cut blow to Hallaron's broad mouth, the soldier twisted the cuffs, applying pressure on Hallaron's captive wrist. The knife slipped from the man's fingers. Grabbing his dazed opponent's right arm, he quickly snapped the cuffs to Hallaron's other wrist.

He heard St. John curse, and from the corner of his eye saw him charge forward. Without releasing his hold on the sergeant, Bolan whirled and shoved Hallaron toward the Juggernaut.

St. John had already launched a karate kick, and he was unable to stop himself when Hallaron appeared in his path. The captain slammed his boot into his NCO's abdomen, dropping him to the floor, where he lay, too winded to move.

The captain turned and took up position, one hand held forward, his other fist balled at hip level. "Now let's see what you've got," he declared.

He jerked his right arm in a feint, shooting his left fist at Bolan's face. The Executioner blocked the man's attacking arm, already swinging his left fist in anticipation of St. John's next move, striking his opponent's forearm before the man could land another punch attack.

Bolan smashed the heel of his palm into the side of St. John's jaw, and the Juggernaut staggered but didn't fall. He turned his head, spit a gob of blood, then faced the Executioner again. He was breathing heavily as he snapped a short kick at the soldier's groin. Bolan managed to block the stroke, but then St. John altered the kick to a high roundhouse aiming for Bolan's head. The Executioner wasn't caught off guard. Grabbing the man's extended leg and shoving hard, he sent St. John toppling.

The captain hit the floor with a thud and the soldier stepped in, delivering a boot heel between the fallen man's splayed legs. St. John screamed in agony. Bolan swiftly grabbed the man's left ankle with his right hand, and, still holding onto his other leg with his left hand, twisted his captive's legs. He succeeded in turning St. John onto his belly. Immediately the Executioner dropped onto the man's shoulder blades, his fists still locked around his opponent's ankles. A version of the "Boston crab," the hold caused terrible pressure on the Juggernaut's lower vertebra as his spine was violently bent backward. Bone crunched and St. John's body went limp.

Hallaron was beginning to recover, and he started to rise from the floor. He got to his knees, extending his cuffed wrists as he clawed for the knife on the ground.

Bolan jumped off St. John's still form and raced toward the sergeant, swinging a kick under Hallaron's ribs before his adversary could grab the knife. The NCO convulsed from the blow as the Executioner moved behind him. Thrusting his arm between the man's legs, Bolan grabbed the short chain that linked

the handcuffs. He yanked hard, pulling both Hallaron's arms between his own legs.

Hallaron found himself folded in two, his head
down, arms immobilized and legs hampered by the
hold. Bolan held on to the cuff chain with one fist
and grabbed the back of the Juggernaut's belt with
the other. He charged for a wall, and Hallaron's skull
connected with the unyielding brick surface. Bolan
heard the crack of bone, and he dropped his opponent
to the floor. He knew Hallaron would no longer be a
problem.

The Executioner didn't waste time congratulating
himself. He picked up the Ka-bar combat knife and
headed for the door. He opened it slowly and peered
into the deserted hallway. The floor was concrete, not
the treacherous tiled surface that concealed Gallow's
electrical shock system. Bolan carefully stepped
forward.

He hugged the wall as he advanced along the corridor, the knife held low. He heard voices as he approached an L-shaped bend. Cautiously he ducked his
head around the corner.

A thick steel door stood ajar, a sign proclaiming
ARMS ROOM in large red letters. Apparently St.
John ran his camp in the traditional manner of a military base—his troops were assigned weapons for use,
but the hardware was kept locked away the rest of
the time.

Bolan crept toward the door. Flattening against the
wall, he peered around the edge of the door to see
inside. A figure stood with his back to Bolan, clad in
Juggernaut armor, a weapon in his hands. His helmet
sat on a table beside him. Another man, dressed in

fatigues, had unlocked a gun rack that contained several 10 mm submachine guns. A pile of loaded magazines for the guns lay on the table. Bolan also spotted his .44 Magnum Desert Eagle and the Beretta 93-R beside the Juggernauts' arsenal.

The Executioner knew he couldn't hope for a better situation. Gripping the knife's handle in one hand, he placed his other palm over the butt to reinforce his blow. The Juggernaut half turned, but before he could raise his weapon, Bolan drove the knife blade into the back of the man's unprotected head, sinking it deep into his brain.

The armor-clad figure collapsed across the table, scattering gun magazines onto the floor. The man in fatigues gaped first at Bolan, then at the knife jammed in the head of his slain comrade. Panicked, he dived across the table, reaching for the Desert Eagle. Bolan grabbed the Juggernaut's helmet, and as the man's fingers closed over the pistol, the Executioner slammed the steel headgear into the center of the guy's face. The man dropped to the floor, blood oozing from his nose and mangled mouth.

The Executioner picked up his Desert Eagle, ejected the magazine to be sure it was loaded, then chambered the first round. He decided to take one of the 10 mm subguns, as well. The weapon was similar in design to an M-3, firing only on full-auto. He loaded the subgun and stuck two spare magazines in his belt.

Bolan resisted the temptation to take the Beretta. He couldn't see the shoulder holster rig, and he knew it would be too awkward to carry the pistol in addition to the other weapons. Sudden footfalls in the hall warned him that he wouldn't be alone for much longer.

Two armed figures, clad in full Juggernaut body armor and helmets, appeared in the hall, headed for the arms room to draw their weapons. The pair came to an abrupt halt when they discovered the Executioner, subgun up and leading. Bolan squeezed the trigger. The recoil drove the subgun into his arms and hip, but the heavy frame and barrel reduced the climb of the weapon. One Juggernaut stopped three projectiles with his breastplate. The soldier hit his companion with another short burst, scoring lethal hits in the Juggernaut's armor and visor.

With his ears ringing painfully from the weapon's report in the enclosed area, the Executioner stepped over the corpses. He continued through the hallway, aware that any hope of stealth had been destroyed. Only one option remained: he had to keep moving and take out anyone who got in his way.

Another Juggernaut appeared as he emerged from the basement level. He drilled the enforcer's body armor with 10 mm piercers, and the corpse toppled sideways, crashing down the basement stairs.

Bolan moved into another corridor. He looked down at the checkerboard floor, realizing the danger as he advanced through the narrow passage.

An armored figure appeared at the end of the corridor. The Juggernaut held a subgun in his gloved fists, but the Executioner triggered his weapon faster. The subgun spit three rounds and the enemy gunman fell across the checkered tiles. Bolan ejected the spent magazine and reached for a full one in his belt.

Andrew Gallow stepped out from around the corner, the remote-control unit aimed at the checkerboard by Bolan's feet. The Executioner dropped his weapon and sprang into the air as electricity crackled from dozens of tiny electrodes in the floor.

Bolan thrust both feet against one wall and shoved his back against the other, the narrow space allowing him to wedge himself between them. Gallow cursed and tossed aside the remote control, clawing at his lab coat pocket for the .45 pistol St. John had given him.

Gallow was no gunfighter. Bolan drew his .44 Magnum pistol, aimed and fired before Gallow could clear the barrel of the Colt from his white coat. The armor-piercing bullet punched through the scientist's chest as if he were made of tissue paper, the force of the slug sending his body sliding across the floor to connect with a wall. Gallow's corpse barely twitched as a scarlet stream began to spread across his chest.

The electrical sizzle from the floor had ceased, rendered inactive the moment Gallow had taken his thumb off the button. Or so Bolan hoped, as, with a deep breath, he dropped down. His boots met innocuous flooring. Scooping up the subgun, he hurried from the corridor.

Bolan reloaded as he headed for the rear door of the building, and emerged from the house. Five figures in Juggernaut armor had assembled by the motor pool. Only two carried submachine guns or side arms. Then a Jeep, with two armed men dressed in fatigues, roared up. The roving patrol had heard the gunfire and rushed to the scene.

The Executioner dealt with the immediate threat first and hosed the patrol with a salvo of bullets, the force of the high-velocity rounds sending them spinning. Blood sprayed from numerous bullet holes as their bodies fell to the ground. A Juggernaut gunman fired back at Bolan's position, but the Executioner had already dropped to a kneeling stance by the doorway. The bullets splintered wood and pierced plaster above his position.

He stayed low, thrusting the gun's barrel around the corner to return fire before the enemy gunman could adjust his aim. The subgun-wielding Juggernaut marched forward, either accustomed to the invulnerability the armor had afforded him, or unaware that Bolan was armed with one of the Juggernauts' weapons. The soldier triggered his weapon, stitching the opponent's breastplate with a line of bullet holes.

One of the pickup trucks roared to life and bolted from the motor pool. Only three Juggernauts remained. Apparently deciding to follow the example of their comrade who'd fled, two of them charged for the other pickup, while the remaining Juggernaut fired his weapon at Bolan. The Executioner was forced to retreat behind the doorway again. He returned fire blindly, trying to keep the enemy from attempting a better plan of attack.

Bolan's subgun hit empty. He swapped magazines and loaded the weapon with the last of his armor-piercing rounds. The enemy gunfire had ceased, and the Executioner peered from the entryway to see the second pickup about to flee. The Juggernaut with the subgun was in the back of the rig, the other two having climbed into the front seat.

The truck rolled from the area as the soldier took aim. He saw the armored figure in the rear of the vehicle raise his weapon. Bolan blasted the gunman with a short salvo, the tumblers knocking the enforcer sideways to topple from the edge of the truck bed and crash to the ground. The pickup kept going, racing for the front gate to the compound.

The Executioner sprinted toward the roving patrol's Jeep. He sprung behind the steering wheel and fired the engine. Setting the submachine gun on the seat beside him, he shifted gears and roared after the two fleeing pickups. The gates stood open wide, the sentries long gone.

Dust churned behind the vehicles as they raced into the night. The trucks had a head start, but Bolan's borrowed Jeep caught up fast. He was trailing the second vehicle, perhaps fifty yards behind, as the three-vehicle caravan headed for an old wooden bridge that spanned the Chattahoochee River.

Bolan aimed his weapon at the rear of the closer truck as the rig rolled across the bridge, triggering a long burst. The bullets raked the fender and tore into a rear tire. Rubber burst and the axle split from the armor-piercing rounds. The truck spun out of control, crashing length-wise into the rail. The wooden barrier gave way on impact and the pickup tumbled into the river. Water washed over the bridge as the Executioner continued his pursuit of the remaining vehicle. He knew the two Juggernauts in the river wouldn't escape: full body armor had a lot of advantages, but preventing a person from drowning was not one of them.

Wailing sirens erupted behind Bolan, and he saw flashing lights in his rearview mirror—a state highway patrol car had joined the chase. The soldier didn't want the cop on his tail, or the local law getting involved. He believed only one Juggernaut was in the truck, but he couldn't be sure that the fugitive was unarmed. In any case, even without a weapon, a lone Juggernaut still posed a lethal problem to police unable to shoot through the body armor. The desperate man could still kill with his steel gauntlets and murderous fists.

The Executioner needed to stop the enemy before the truck reached the city. He drew closer to the speeding vehicle and unleashed another salvo. Bullets tore into the road and punctured the metal gate at the rear of the pickup. A chunk of rubber spewed from a tire, and the truck swerved before it was brought under control.

Bolan noticed that the highway patrol car had pulled onto the shoulder of the road some distance behind him, the cop probably deciding not to tangle with someone firing a submachine gun at a moving vehicle. The enemy truck kept going, even though it appeared to be hobbled by a flat tire. Smoke rose from the torn rubber, but the rig still raced toward the city lights.

A cluster of trees briefly blocked Bolan's view, but then he caught sight of the truck as it screamed onto an exit ramp. The soldier made the turn and followed the pickup's path. It had pulled into the parking lot of a minimall, halting near the self-serve gasoline pumps in front of the small store. Bolan followed, stopping the Jeep behind the truck. The subgun was out of ammo. He climbed from the vehicle and drew the Desert Eagle from hip leather.

With the pistol up and leading, he approached the rig. No one appeared to be in the cab of the vehicle.

He circled the rear, but that, too, was clear. He scanned the area, noticing an air pump near the pickup and a column of decorative shrubs that extended to the corner of the minimall.

Bushes rustled and suddenly parted. The Juggernaut rushed forward, and Bolan swung his pistol toward him. A long, flexible black object streaked out, striking Bolan's hand. The .44 Magnum pistol fell from his grasp, and the Juggernaut raised his arm to deliver another stroke with his improvised weapon.

Bolan jumped back to avoid the attack. He glimpsed the weapon in his opponent's gloved fist. It was a length of hose, probably ripped from the air pump. The Juggernaut approached, featureless behind the visored mask of his helmet. Light from the glass doors and windows of the store fell across the combatants as the Juggernaut swung the hose again.

The Executioner ducked his head and raised his arms to meet the attack. The rubber whip connected, stinging his forearm. Bolan's hands flashed and he snared the hose, pulling with all his strength. The Juggernaut was jerked forward, before he reacted, tugging with equal might.

Bolan suddenly released his hold on the rubber tubing. The Juggernaut staggered backward, propelled by his own momentum. He released the hose and flailed his heavy arms as he tried to maintain his balance. The Executioner charged, leaping forward and driving a boot into the center of his opponent's chest. The Juggernaut crashed through the door of the store, glass shattering as he toppled inside and fell onto the floor.

"Sweet Jesus!" a voice exclaimed.

Bolan barely glanced at the astonished youth behind the counter. A woman customer dropped a container of milk and retreated to the end of the store. A man with a straw Stetson hat stood frozen by a magazine rack, his eyes wide and mouth agape. The armored figure rolled onto all fours and tried to rise as Bolan stepped through the opening that had been the door. Pieces of glass crunched under his boots as he stepped forward, delivering a hard kick to the Juggernaut's helmeted head.

His foot seemed to bounce off the metal surface. The Juggernaut's head barely moved. Bolan slammed a boot heel to the center of the visor, the impact jarring the muscles of his leg. Instantly the Juggernaut slashed a steel-covered arm at Bolan's legs, but he whirled out of reach and swung his boot again.

"Get out of here!" the clerk yelled. "I mean it! Take it outside!"

Bolan ignored them as he circled his opponent. The Juggernaut had managed to get one foot flat on the floor, and the soldier knew that he would be upright in a second. He slammed his heel into the riveted top of the visor. The Juggernaut's head snapped back and the helmet flew off. Raymond Stylles stared up at the Executioner.

"Now it's my turn, Stylles," Bolan said.

Stylles suddenly thrust his left arm forward, driving his fist into Bolan's abdomen. The punch felt like a battering ram, and it sent the Executioner crashing backward into a display of plastic soft drink bottles. Bolan staggered across the room, winded by the punishing blow. He felt something wet and warm under his torn shirt, and he realized he had been cut by the steel spikes on the Juggernaut's fist.

"It might be over for me," Stylles snarled as he rose from the floor, "but it's the end of the line for you, too."

He stepped toward Bolan and drew back a deadly steel fist. The Executioner swiftly jabbed with his left, smashing into Stylles's face and drawing blood from his nose. Furiously, the Juggernaut swung a left hook, Bolan weaving away from the studded fist just in time.

"I triggered the alarm!" the clerk shouted. "The cops are coming!"

Stylles threw a right cross. His armor-heavy limb was dangerous, but slow. Bolan dodged the punch and hooked his left, hitting the Juggernaut on the cheekbone. The renegade groaned as he lashed out, his arm extended in a wide sweep. His steel-encased limb hit Bolan with enough power to force the soldier against the glass-fronted door of a refrigerator.

Stylles charged and launched a kick for Bolan's abdomen. At the last second, Bolan sidestepped, and the Juggernaut's steel boot crashed through the glass, exploding a couple of cans of beer. Stylles cursed as he tried to dislodge his foot.

Bolan moved behind his opponent, and, swinging his arms forward, locked them together in a viselike grip around the Juggernaut's neck.

Bone crunched as Bolan twisted his captive's head, then let him crash to the floor. His head lay at an impossible angle, his eyes glassy, a dumbfounded expression on his face.

Bolan headed for the door. He gestured to the clerk as he stepped through the shattered threshold.

"The police will take care of the mess."

A GREEN HONDA ACCORD rolled to a stop by the curb on Martin Luther King Jr. Drive, and Bolan emerged from the shadows. Leo Turrin opened the passenger-side door, and the Executioner slid into the seat beside the little Fed.

"How'd it go?" Bolan asked as he shut the door.

"The security camera in the minimall filmed your fight with that Juggernaut," Turrin replied. "Pretty exciting stuff. Bet I could sell it to one of the tabloid news shows for a bundle."

"So have you got it?"

Turrin picked up a videocassette tape from the floor and handed it over. "I convinced the clerk and the local police to let the Justice Department have it. Unfortunately it'll get erased when somebody gets an electromagnet too close to the tape. We can't have your face showing up on the evening news. By the way, Hal contacted me about a report from a NSA SIGINT satellite that passed over the compound. Apparently the sensor surveillance gear detected a very high heat level in a building toward the center of the compound. It appeared to be some sort of industrial furnace."

"The barn," Bolan replied, "of course. They needed somewhere to forge metal for their weapons and body armor."

Turrin glanced at the spots of blood on Bolan's shirt, and asked, "You okay, Striker?"

"Hell," Bolan said, "I've had a lot worse than this. I'm just ready to go home."

"That's exactly where we're headed," Turrin assured him.

Don't miss out on the action in these titles!

Deathlands

#62534	STONEFACE	$5.50 U.S.	☐
		$6.50 CAN.	☐
#62535	BITTER FRUIT	$5.50 U.S.	☐
		$6.50 CAN.	☐
#62536	SKYDARK	$5.50 U.S.	☐
		$6.50 CAN.	☐

The Destroyer

#63220	SCORCHED EARTH	$5.50 U.S.	☐
		$6.50 CAN.	☐
#63221	WHITE WATER	$5.50 U.S.	☐
		$6.50 CAN.	☐
#63222	FEAST OR FAMINE	$5.50 U.S.	☐
		$6.50 CAN.	☐

(limited quantities available on certain titles)

TOTAL AMOUNT	$
POSTAGE & HANDLING	$
($1.00 for one book, 50¢ for each additional)	
APPLICABLE TAXES*	$_____
TOTAL PAYABLE	$_____
(check or money order—please do not send cash)	

To order, complete this form and send it, along with a check or money order for the total above, payable to Gold Eagle Books, to: **In the U.S.:** 3010 Walden Avenue, P.O. Box 9077, Buffalo, NY 14269-9077; **In Canada:** P.O. Box 636, Fort Erie, Ontario, L2A 5X3.

Name:_____

Address:_____ City:_____

State/Prov.:_____ Zip/Postal Code:_____

*New York residents remit applicable sales taxes.
 Canadian residents remit applicable GST and provincial taxes.

GEBACK19A

The body most people would die for...

#109 American Obsession

Created by
WARREN MURPHY
and RICHARD SAPIR

A futuristic hormone treatment instantly giving the jet-set the bodies they've always wanted seems too good to be true... Soon innocent people pay the price for a killer diet, and the House of Sinanju takes on an army of celebrities and a greedy corporation.

Look for it in October wherever Gold Eagle books are sold.

A violent struggle for survival in a post-holocaust world

JAMES AXLER
DEATH LANDS®
Watersleep

In the altered reality of the Deathlands, America's coastal waters haven't escaped the ravages of the nukecaust, but the awesome power of the oceans still rules there. It's a power that will let Ryan Cawdor, first among post-holocaust survivors, ride the crest of victory—or consign his woman to the raging depths.
